KALAMAS AND ACHERON
RIVERS OF HADES

Other translations of Greek fiction from Colenso Books

Konstantinos Theotokis, *The life and death of Hangman Thomas* (2016),
Corfiot Tales (2017),
What price honour? – The convict: two novellas (2020)
all translated and introduced by J. M. Q. Davies.

Original fiction in English from Colenso Books

Lawrence Durrell, *The Placebo*,
edited by Richard Pine and David Roessel (2018)

Jim Potts, *This spinning world: 43 stories from far and wide* (2019)

Louisa Adjoa Parker, *Stay with me* (stories, 2020)

Leslie Retallick, *Before the fire* (a novel, 2021)

Mark Allen, *Life Term* (a novel, expected March 2021)

CHRISTOPHOROS MILIONIS was born in 1932 in the village of Peristeri in the Pogoni district of Epirus (northwestern Greece). The village is about 40km northwest of Ioannina (or Yannena, as he calls it in this book). Though his early education was disrupted by the Axis Occupation, he did attend a secondary school in Ioannina and later studied Classics at the Aristotelian University of Thessaloniki. From 1955 to 1991 he had a career in education, as teacher, headmaster and school advisor, and played a role in the selection of Modern Greek literary texts for inclusion in the secondary school curricula. His first story was published in 1954. The stories in this collection were first published between 1976 and 1990. The collection itself (without the story "Phryni") was first published in 1985 and awarded the State Short Story Prize in the following year. Milionis published several more collections of short stories and a number of novels. He died in January 2017.

MARJORIE CHAMBERS was born in Dromore, County Down, Northern Ireland and educated at Trinity College Dublin and the Sorbonne. She taught Modern Greek language and literature at Queen's University Belfast. Her translations of Greek poetry, prose and drama were first published in journals and books in the USA, Greece, the UK and Ireland, and have now been collected and republished (with some previously unpublished poetry translations) by Colenso Books as noted below. She died at her home in Holywood, County Down in March 2019.

OTHER TRANSLATIONS BY MARJORIE CHAMBERS FROM COLENSO BOOKS

Iakovos Kambanellis, *Three plays: The courtyard of wonders; The four legs of the table; Ibsenland* (2015)

Yannis Ritsos among his contemporaries: twentieth-century Greek poetry, by Yannis Ritsos, George Vafopoulos, Nikos Gatsos, Nikiforos Vrettakos, Miltos Sachtouris and Yannis Kondos (2018)

Panayotis Tranoulis, *Keratochori: my life in the furnace* (2021)

KALAMAS AND ACHERON

RIVERS OF HADES

BY

CHRISTOPHOROS MILIONIS

TRANSLATED FROM THE GREEK
BY
MARJORIE CHAMBERS

EDITED BY

ANTHONY HIRST AND PATRICK SAMMON

COLENSO BOOKS
2021

This revised translation first published January 2021 by
Colenso Books
68 Palatine Road, London N16 8ST, UK
colensobooks@gmail.com

ISBN 978-1-912788-07-1

Translation, Translator's Preface and some notes
Copyright © 2021 The Estate of Marjorie Chambers

"Introduction", note on "Transliteration and punctuation",
"An alphabetical list of Greek personal and place names . . ."
and footnotes marked "(Eds)" Copyright © 2021 Colenso Books

Published by permission of Tatiana Milioni and Dafni Milioni

An earlier version of this translation was first published
as *Kalamás and Achéron* (Athens: Kedros Publishers, 1996).

This collection of stories was first published in Greek as *Καλαμάς κι Αχέροντας*, without the story "Phryni" (Athens: Στιγμή, 1985), republished, including "Phryni" (Athens: Κέδρος, 1990) and again, with authorial corrections (Athens: Κίχλη, 2017).
Copyright © 2017 Εκδόσεις Κίχλη & Τατιάνα Μηλιώνη

The "Translator's Preface" was first published as "Translating Milionis", in Greek translation in *Θέματα Λογοτεχνίας* 23 (2003).
The original English version is published here for the first time, by permission of Christos Alexiou.

The image on the front cover is derived from a colour photograph by Jim Potts. It shows the River Acheron at a location, close to its source, sometimes known as "The Gates of Hades".

CONTENTS

Introduction	vii
Transliteration and pronunciation	x
Acknowledgements 1996 and 2021	xiii
Translator's Preface	xv
The toad	1
Kalamas and Acheron	9
The hoopoe	21
Big Mother	29
Koriandolino	37
My childhood friend, Ismail Kadare	47
"Symphonia"	57
Phryni	69
The last tanner	77
That piper	87
From generation to generation	97
An alphabetical list of Greek personal and place names and other Greek words, with the stressed syllables marked	106

INTRODUCTION

The distinguished translator, Marjorie Chambers, died on the 25th of March 2019. *Kalamas and Acheron: rivers of Hades* is one of two collections of connected and largely autobiographical Greek short stories translated by Marjorie Chambers and now republished by Colenso Books. The other is *Keratochori: my life in the furnace* by Panayotis Tranoulis. The original intention was to launch the two books at a memorial event close to the first anniversary of her death. This had to be postponed because of restrictions on gatherings in response to the early stages of the Covid-19 pandemic. It was rescheduled for November 2020 but that date too proved impossible; and it is not certain when such events will become feasible once more. The two books are now being issued in advance of the second anniversary of Marjorie's death.

During the last months of her life Marjorie and I discussed the republication of these two volumes of fiction, to complete the publication or republication of all her translations of Modern Greek literature. Colenso Books had already published her translations of *Three Plays* by Iakovos Kambanellis (2015) and a collection of all of her translations of Greek poetry with the title *Yannis Ritsos among his contemporaries: twentieth-century Greek poetry* (2018).

The present translation was first published in 1996, as *Kalamás and Achéron* (now out of print), by the Athens publishing house Kedros in their Modern Greek Writers series of English translations of Greek prose texts — mostly fiction. The published text contained a few errors, which Marjorie marked in a copy of the book which she sent to me. Apart from correcting these errors and a several more which I and my co-editor Patrick Sammon noted, the main changes we have made are in the transliteration of Greek personal and place names. The system of transliteration — imposed, we believe, by the Greek editors at Kedros — was not as useful a guide to pronunciation for English speakers as it might have been. The letter *gamma* for example is always represented as *gh* even where it is pronounced as a Y. We have substituted a more phonetic system, as outlined in the note on "Transliteration and Pronunciation" that follows.

In the Kedros version most of the personal and place names carried an acute accent to indicate where the stress falls. We decided not to replicate this practice as names occur frequently both in narrative and in dialogue and the presence of multiple accented words on almost every page would make the text appear unnecessarily strange. Instead, for those who want to know where the stress falls, we have listed all the names that occur in these stories, and in some of the footnotes, at the back of the book, with each name broken up into syllables and with the stressed syllable in bold type.

One systematic change we have made — and this does go against Marjorie's practice (and that of other translators, and of some novelists writing conversations among Greeks in English) — is to eliminate the use of the Greek vocative case when one Greek is addressing another in dialogue. It applies only to male names and consists in almost all cases of dropping the final S of the nominative, so that, for example, "Nikos" becomes "Niko" and "Vangelis" becomes "Vangeli" when a Nikos or a Vangelis is addressed by another character. As no one translating into English uses the Greek genitive or accusative forms where they occur in Greek, we see no compelling reason to use the vocative either; it amounts in fact to a mixing of two languages. However, in the names of streets, where, in Greek, a word for "Street" or "Avenue" etc. is followed by the name in the genitive, the genitive form is, by convention, retained in English, following the way street names are transliterated on signs in Greek cities, so that, to take examples from this book, what translates as the "Street of Patmos" is rendered as *Patmou Street* and not *Patmos Street*; and the "Avenue of Alexandra" is *Alexandras Avenue* and not *Alexandra Avenue*. Another exception must be made for those surnames which are always in the genitive case, and surnames of women which are by convention in the genitive case of the surname of the woman's father or husband.

INTRODUCTION

The text has many references to the political situation and the living conditions in Greece during the Axis Occupation of the Second World War, and the Greek Civil War that followed. The Kedros publication had eight pages of notes at the back of the book and an asterisk in the text indicated the presence of a note. As the majority of these notes will be needed immediately by many readers if they are to understand implications and references in the text, we have placed them instead as footnotes. We are not sure that Marjorie was the author or sole author of all of these notes and we have edited them freely, removing information that seemed unnecessary and adding other details which we felt were lacking. We have also provided some entirely new notes of our own, and these are marked "(Eds)" at the end. They are most numerous in "My childhood friend Ismail Kadare", where all the quotations from Kadare's novel *The General of the Dead Army* have been identified, with page references to the English translation published by Vintage.

We have added the subtitle, *rivers of Hades*, to make the significance of the main title, *Kalamas and Acheron*, clearer to English readers who may not be familiar with the names of these rivers in Epirus. Of course, only the Acheron is, in Greek mythology, a river of Hades, the route to the Underworld. The pairing of the Kalamas and the Acheron — or their identification, as though there was one river with two names — derives from a Greek mistranslation of a line from Byron's *Childe Harold's Pilgrimage* (see page 9, especially the footnote, and also page 12). However, the pairing is significant since both rivers are associated with another kind of Hell: the battles and atrocities of the Axis Occupation and the Greek Civil War that followed. Memories of such events play a vital role in the interpenetration of past and present which is a key theme in the eleven closely connected stories that make up this volume.

Anthony Hirst
January 2021

TRANSLITERATION AND PRONUNCIATION

There are over 270 Greek personal names, place names, or other Greek words to be found in these stories. The transliteration system presented here is designed to give as clear as possible an indication for English speakers of the sounds of Greek words, while preserving Greek spelling as far as is consistent with this aim. To simplify further, for example by using *f* instead of *ph* for the Greek letter *phi*, or *h* instead of *ch* for the Greek letter *chi*, would obscure the connections with English words derived from Ancient Greek; the same goes for retaining *ei* and vocalic *y*, rather than replacing them by *i*, even though all three have the same sound.

The following notes are not about the pronunciation of Greek letters as such, but about the pronunciation of the English letters which we have used to represent them.

Vowels

There are only five vowel *sounds* in Greek, represented as follows:

a represents a slightly variable sound somewhere between short *a* in *rat* and long *a* in *rather*.

e is always short as in *get*. There are no silent vowels in Greek and **e** at the end of the word is always sounded.

i, **ei**, and **y** all represent the same slightly variable sound, between *i* in *fit* and *ee* in *feet* (usually closer to the latter). However, when **y** is the first letter of a word and is followed by another vowel, or occurs in the middle of a word between two vowels, it acts as a consonant and has the value of *y* in *yet* or *royal* (and usually represents the combination of Greek letters *gamma-iota*, or an initial *iota* followed by another unstressed vowel).

o is always short as in *rot*.

ou represents the sound *oo* in *root*.

Apart from **ei** and **ou** all other consecutive vowels must be pronounced separately as parts of different syllables. Where they would be likely to be run together by English speakers the diaeresis has been used; for example Siëmos is three syllables (Si-e-mos) and Sabethaï is four (Sa-be-tha-i).

Consonants

Although double consonants occur in Greek, and are retained in this book in transliterated Greek, the doubling has no effect on pronunciation. Most of the consonants and combinations of consonants have more or less the same sound as they have in English, but the following should be noted:

ch represents the Greek letter *chi*, a rough throaty sound as in German *machen* or *Bach*, or Scottish *loch*. It is never like *ch* in *change*. Some people prefer to represent the letter *chi* by **h**, but this produces some very strange results, as for example "Hristos", the Greek word from which "Christ" derives, though the English word is pronounced as if the Greek had been "Kristos" rather than "Christos". If the guttural sound is difficult **k** is probably a better fallback than **h**.

d is problematic. In the middle of words it should be pronounced like the thick *th* in *rather*, unless preceded by **n**, in which case the pronunciation is a hard *d* as in *candy*. At the beginning of a word it may be either soft (as *th* in *rather*) or hard in names or other words which Greek has borrowed from other languages.

dz – when followed by **z**, **d** is always hard whether **n** precedes it or not.

f – see under **ph** below.

g is always hard as in *get* never soft as in *gel* no matter what vowel follows, and even when preceded by **n**. This is something of an oversimplification, since the Greek letter *gamma* when followed by vowels **a**, **o** and **ou** is a much more guttural sound (formed in the throat) than the English hard g (which in Greek requires the combination of *gamma* and *kappa*). No attempt is made here to distinguish between guttural **g** and hard **g**.

ph represents the Greek letter *phi* for which many people prefer to use **f**. Most English words containing *ph* pronounced as *f* are derived from Greek, and this is a good reason for using **ph** in transliterated Greek. Where **f** is used in transliteration of Greek words in this book it represents the Greek letter *ypsilon* (otherwise represented by **y** or the **u** in **ou**) which becomes consonantal when it follows **a** or **e**, and the combinations are pronounced either as **af** /**ef** (with *f* as in *if*, not as in *of*) or as **av** /**ev**, depending on what sound follows.

ps – the **p** is always pronounced even at the beginning of a word, never dropped as in the English pronunciation of *psychology*.

s is always pronounced as in *sing* or *list*, even at the end of a word where English usually requires *ss* to avoid the Z-sound: *hostess*; compare *ours* or *horses*. (Before certain other consonants the Greek S does take on the Z-sound, but no examples of this occur in these stories.)

th is always thin as in the words *thin*, *thick* and *bath*, never thick as in *this* or *bathing* (see also **d** above).

ts occurs naturally in the middle of Greek words but it only occurs at the beginning of words borrowed from other languages. Even at the beginning of a word the **t** should be sounded.

y – see under **i** above.

x is always pronounced as if it were the combination **ks** even at the beginning of a word; it is never reduced to **z** as in the English pronunciation of *xylophone*.

As already noted in the Introduction, there is, at the back of the book, an alphabetical list of all the Greek names or other Greek words that occur in the main text of this book and in some footnotes. The words are divided into syllables and the stressed syllable is printed in bold.

ACKNOWLEDGEMENTS

I wish to express my thanks to Despina Galanouli who gave generously of her time when consulted, also to my son Michael Chambers, for his sensitive and careful help in refining the language, and for producing and proof-reading the typescript, and not least to the author Christophoros Milionis, who so willingly and patiently co-operated with me, and provided much valuable information.

Marjorie Chambers, 1996

I too would like to thank Michael Chambers, as well as Christos Alexiou, for their help in providing contacts and determining the permissions necessary for the republication of this translation; and to further thank Christos Alexiou for permission to use as the Preface a short essay by Marjorie Chambers which was first published (in Greek translation) in a journal that he edits. Above all I thank Tatiana Milioni, widow of the author, Christophoros Milionis (who died in 2017), and a friend of Marjorie Chambers, for her gracious permission for the republication of this translation in a slightly revised form. My thanks also to Michelle McGaughey for her careful retyping of the eleven stories in preformatted files so that no further typesetting was required; to my co-editor Patrick Sammon; and to Jim Potts for providing the photograph (originally in colour) that appears on the front cover.

Anthony Hirst, January 2021

TRANSLATOR'S PREFACE

This essay was first published as "Translating Milionis", in Greek translation in *Θέματα Λογοτεχνίας* (*Literary Matters*) 23 (August 2003) and the original English version is published here by permission of the editor of that journal, Christos Alexiou.

I was lucky to have been asked to translate this volume of short stories by Christophoros Milionis, as I feel I can lay claim to certain credentials which facilitate my understanding of the village community in Epirus where Milionis was brought up. I too grew up in a rural community, in Northern Ireland, where my mother, like the author's father, was the primary-school teacher. More importantly, my being Irish gives me, perhaps, a particularly sympathetic insight into the author's experience.

In an article in the journal *In Other Words*, the translator Kay Cicellis, writing about the difficulties of translating Modern Greek into English, comments on the historical and political divergence between Greece and Britain. This divergence is, I believe, much less pronounced in Ireland. Both Greece and Ireland were occupied for centuries and have suffered ongoing political troubles since the establishment of the Kingdom of Greece in 1830 and the Irish Free State in 1922 (which made permanent the partition of Ireland).

As a consequence of our similar histories, we Irish are perhaps close to Greeks in our more cynical attitude towards politics, and in our personal behaviour and customs. For example, the various subtle nuances of class distinction in England, fostered over centuries of peace, are unknown in Ireland, and in Greece too, I would say.

In Greece and Ireland, however, we have our own less subtle nuances to reckon with. The experience of political division, which in both countries has led to civil war, is an experience all too familiar to an Irish translator of Greek.

In the title story, "Kalamas and Acheron", Milionis, in laconic mode, recalls his prolonged efforts to find a teaching post, treading warily through the minefield of suspicion and mistrust that lingered after the Civil War.

The sense of alienation and loneliness too, a legacy of the previous traumatic events, is movingly evoked in "The hoopoe". The clerk, whose health has been impaired by the German Occupation, at last finds a job and goes on his holiday to an island. At the sight of German tourists in a taverna he relives the burning of his village. Milionis' skill in sliding in and out of the past is particularly effective here in exposing the rawness of the searing memories.

The author's finely tuned ear for dialogue is at its most acute in "The last tanner" where he describes a wake, a custom that is still practised in rural parts of Ireland, especially in the Irish-speaking areas of Donegal and Sligo.[1] The tanner's friends keep an all-night vigil over his coffin, drinking raki and singing folksongs. In their fond remembrances of the old days, when the tanners were kings in the village, the mourners also lament a way of life that has gone.

In "Symphonia", the author's friendship with Mitsos Doulias, an ELAS[2] fighter, is quite enchanting. The child feels something approaching awe for the simple man who lives by his socialist principles, and tells him stories from his Communist booklets, as they sit gazing towards Albania. Years later the author finds him in a sad refugee village in Hungary.

But the sense of loss that echoes in these stories is perhaps most poignant in "My childhood friend, Ismail Kadare". Milionis

---

[1] The custom probably still exists in the counties of Tyrone and Fermanagh in Northern Ireland. Tunes associated with the mourning ceased to be used after the 1930s; they are remembered now only by the travelling people. Professional mourners and friends sit by the coffin all night, two nights if the death occurs before sunset. The body must not be left alone; prayers and words extolling the dead person ease their transition into the afterlife. I am indebted for this information to Professor Dónall Ó Baoill (Donal O'Boyle), Writer-in-Residence, Celtic Studies, Queen's University Belfast.

[2] The National Popular Liberation Army.

feels a kinship with the Albanian writer, recalling their common experience of the Italian invasion, and the coming and going between Albanian villages and villages in his townland,[3] the indistinct mountain border being generally ignored. In 1944, however, the border was clearly defined with barbed wire fences and heavy patrols.

In remembering his village, Milionis evokes its poverty and its earthy smells. He recalls "Big Mother", who had the village in thrall to her cornflour pudding and the bread she baked; the grieving old woman known as "The toad", who is taunted by the village children; the delectable "Phryni" in a bucolic scene where he weaves baskets with her amidst the lush, shady greenery of the ravine.

Although my own childhood experience of rural life in Ireland was ten years further on — it was physically somewhat more comfortable than in Milionis' village of Peristeri — the eccentric characters, the sometimes atavistic behaviour, the unlikely friendships are constant everywhere and at all times in such communities. I still remember with delight a tall, skinny, attractive farmer's wife who loved the poetry of Robert Burns and would milk her cows in a fur coat and sling-back sandals.

But in Milionis' stories the other landscape, the dark landscape of the river Acheron, the mythical river of Hades, is never far from his mind. Yet despite the burned villages, the devastated country, the misplaced trust and hopes ruined, and — in recent decades — exquisite islands despoiled by tourism, the story "That piper", a loving tribute to Papadiamandis,[4] reaffirms our faith that the spirit of a nation endures in its literature.

Marjorie Chambers

---

[3] A townland is the smallest division of land in Ireland; it need not contain a town. (Eds)
[4] See page 87, note 1. (Eds)

The toad

After the Occupation[1] came other disasters. People were scattered, and the country was ruined. Exactly thirty-nine years have gone by, Triandaphyllos and myself reckoned, when he came last summer as a tourist from Stockholm with his wife and their son. Let's say forty. Forty years — a great, dark chasm. Yet it can be bridged with one leap by a repulsive little animal, the *ziamba*.

In our part of the country — up there between Mourgana and Kasidiaris — *ziamba* was the name we gave to the *toad* — if this word is more comprehensible. I don't know what else I can do, since things forsake us one by one, and their names become buried in a heap in the stockpiles of our dictionaries. So, there's no other way than for me to describe the animal as we do to little children who haven't seen much because of their age.

The toad then, commonly known as *ziamba*, is a kind of dry land frog. It's as big as a fist, fat, short-necked and ugly, with puffy cheeks, swollen eyes and yellowish skin covered in pimples. It lives alone in its damp, dark hole, beneath old tiles, at the back of the house, where the dirty water from the sink is stagnant with scraps of food, rotten tomato pickle and whey, as well as ashes of lye. If you so much as lift the tile and uncover him, he rolls up and stays motionless, confidently expecting to deceive you in this way. Utterly stupid of course. It brings to mind the instructions they gave us at the Military Training Centre in Corinth, on "cover and camouflage" in the event of nuclear or chemical warfare. If you can overcome your disgust and touch him with a stick,

---

[1] The Axis Occupation of Greece, April 1941 – October 1944, involving German, Italian and Bulgarian forces. (Eds)

those numerous pimples on his skin vomit a dirty, milky liquid — sheer poison. Now that I think about it, I realise that from many points of view the toad is the most common type of animal in Athens today: the Athenian Toad, hiding in his cramped hole of an apartment, in Lord knows what filth, or skulking about in his four-wheeled lair, ready to dart his poison at you the moment he suspects he is being threatened.

But at that time, we called an old woman in our neighbourhood the *ziamba*. This was unjust and irrational, and could only be excused, perhaps, by our childish cruelty, inexperience and irresponsibility. She was a short-necked old woman, with a broad face half-covered by her dirty headscarf, and she had protruding eyes. Her hut was the last of the houses in our neighbourhood. It was buried in nettles and sorrel that sprouted among the rusty oil cans and rotten floor cloths that my aunt, Amia-Miya,[2] would throw out the window of her wash house. There, one could also see bloodstained cotton wool and bits of cloth, because my aunt, as I heard later, suffered from frequent haemorrhages. This was the reason she remained childless. My aunt's house, built around 1900 with the gold sovereigns that my uncle Aryiris brought back from Constantinople — or the City[3] as we called it — was big and imposing — a "gentleman's residence" as tourists from the provinces would call it today. It had many rooms, which were intended to house the dynasty that my uncle probably reckoned on sowing, when he came down every two years from the City, as was his custom. But it seems that things turned out differently for

---

[2] "Amia" is a Turkish word for "aunt", used for Miya because she had lived for many years in Constantinople (Istanbul).
[3] As the capital of the Byzantine Empire and its spiritual centre, *Konstandinoupolis* (Constantinople) was commonly referred to, and still often is referred to, simply as *i Polis* (the City).

him. The rooms remained closed up, and my aunt childless. Her nephews, in other words ourselves, visited her whenever parcels arrived from the City before the war — tins of butter, rose-coloured Turkish Delight (the large size), rice and sugar. We would address her as "Amia-Miya", a salutation of the City, which for us epitomised all the reverence and all the magic that her possessions radiated, and who knows what greatness she was reminded of. In the end, neither the thick walls of the house, nor the high fence at the front of it, with the big covered carriage entrance, escaped the Germans' fire. But this happened a short while later.

Anyway, behind Aryirena's[4] house was the old woman's hut. She lived in there, invisible, day and night, or so everybody else thought. We neighbours, on the other hand, knew that she would go through the alleyway at dawn, pulling an ancient cow, skeletal and dirty, and come back late in the evening, dragging herself along, bent double. Often, at that hour, Amia-Miya would call her to the window of the washroom and give her a plate of food or a cup of sugar, and a little Indian tea for her cough. She would take it secretively, and withdraw to her hut. And then, in the breathless silence that weighed on the village when night fell, you could hear a soft lament, during which every so often there would be a long, lingering cry: "My Michalis! My Michalis!" Then, it would evaporate into a dry cough, stifled and submerged. But nobody else heard this, because nobody had any reason to come near that hut.

Once a year, on New Year's Eve, the children — the village had children then — and of course myself among them, would arrive at the end of the village towards midnight, and bang on her door as if we were going to sing

---

[4] Aryirena is a more formal name for the narrator's aunt, Amia-Miya, formed from her husband's first name, Aryiris (see page 2).

carols for Saint Basil.⁵ We wouldn't wait for a response. We would move off further down the street, and sing,

Here's the horn-owl's nest, the vampire's hole . . .

until the door would creak half open, allowing a trembling reflection from the fireplace to appear. Incomprehensible cries and curses could be heard, swept away by the shouts and trampling feet of the children, who would run scattering into the darkness.

So the year ended happily for us, and the old woman would go back into her hole, bolting the door on the inside.

Nobody would go near her hut again, until, that is, the Germans set out from the ends of the earth, from the Oder and the Rhine, and burnt it down, along with the other poor houses and Amia-Miya's mansion.

Just before that invasion, a strange activity took hold of the village. The villagers were digging in their orchards and fields, and burying their kitchen utensils, or entire trunks of clothes and barrels of wheat. Others were moving *kilims*⁶ and bridal eiderdowns to out-of-the-way hiding places. Then they would think they weren't safe there, so they would dig them up and take them somewhere else. In other words, there was panic and confusion. When it got dark, they went away from the village and hid in the forests and ravines, then came back after a few days to find everything burnt to the ground.

It was then that my aunt Aryirena started a quarrel with the old woman — they were equal now, since neither had anything left. My aunt said she had hidden in a pile of stones, among the nettles and sorrel, a pitcher with butter in it, taken

---

⁵ It is the custom for children to go round the houses singing carols on New Year's Eve, which is also the eve of Saint Basil's Day.
⁶ Woven rugs of the type often referred to as Turkish carpets, used as wall hangings as well as floor coverings. (Eds)

from the tins that her husband used to send her from the City, and now it wasn't there. "Here's the hole I put it in, ladies, and here are the footprints on the ashes near it." The old woman must have seen her hiding it, and then when she came back and found her hut burnt down, she dug it out and took it. "It's obvious, ladies. She came back to the village in the morning, and I returned in the afternoon." My aunt, faced with the magnitude of her misfortune, had lost all sense of proportion. She was projecting everything onto that pitcher. Beside herself with rage, she reminded the old woman of the presents she gave her, and how kind she was to her, giving her food and drink every evening from her window — and all this in a strange, hoarse voice. The old woman just said, "Poison would be better than this," and didn't speak again. Pulling her cow along, coughing and bent over, she took the path and headed for the stream at Rouvelas Cave, where, a short time later, we found her dead.

Just at that time, the first snow had fallen in our area. People were shivering in their makeshift huts with the dry stone walls and straw roofs, their eyes swollen and filled with smoke, like ferrets. Perhaps that was why the idea occurred to Triandaphyllos and myself to go to Rouvelas Cave and smoke out the fox. We knew her lair was a hollow with two openings, one of them at the back of the cave, and the other a few steps away at the base of the rock, where there was a bush. Her tracks could be seen on the ground, where she went in and out. We had located the place in the summer when we were hunting wild pigeon, but decided to wait until the winter when foxskin would be worth something. Over the exit by the bush we would fix a sack made from an Italian soldier's cape, which we'd bring there filled with straw, and light a fire with the straw just inside the other entrance to the lair, the one from the back of the cave. The main thing would be to close the sack with both hands as soon as the fox rushed into it, panicked by the smoke. Triandaphyllos, who was bolder and stronger than me, had undertaken to do this job. I would then smash its bones to pieces with the heavy stick that I was using at that time as a support so as not to slip in my wooden shoes. The sun had come out, and the snow was blinding us. It was still snowing, however, on the Mourgana mountains. The cold stung our dry cheeks, and our hands were numb, so that we worried more about lighting a fire than about the value of the foxskin.

When we arrived at Rouvelas, we found the old woman huddled up at the back of the cave, wrapped to the top of her head in a dirty army blanket. We uncovered her, and her face appeared, with eyes open and toothless mouth gaping. A short distance away, her cow was grazing on the lower branches of the trees. Usual things that didn't surprise us.

The next day, I heard something about Michalis too. The conversation turned to him in the porch of the church, where five or six neighbours had lit a fire to keep themselves warm after the burial. Minas the gravedigger, a crazy man who always wore his flat cap askew, above his right ear, asked if they would be handing round *kollyva*.[7] Old Bindos said to him, "Who has the old woman got to hand round the *kollyva*?" and "Who has any wheat to boil?" Minas lifted up his cap, and took out an old photograph. "The women found it in her bosom," he said, "when they were arranging the body."

The photograph was passed from hand to hand. It was creased and soiled, but the figures were still visible. "The one in the hospital clothes is Michalis. The other must be an Italian." He was a tall young man, exhausted looking, and he was leaning his head on the foreigner's shoulder. Old Bindos

---

[7] Dishes of boiled wheat decorated with nuts, raisins, etc. often arranged in patterns, eaten by family and guests at funerals and memorial services. (Eds)

said that the deceased had sent Michalis to Constantinople at the age of seventeen, to work in Aryiris' tannery. "He fell ill there, and they put him into a sanatorium. Then they loaded him onto an Italian ship. He was to be taken off at Piraeus, where he could find fellow villagers working as waiters in the cook shops. They would send him to the village, for a change of air. Maybe he arrived, or maybe he didn't. Who knows? The blockade[8] was on. Hunters found the photograph later, near the main road. It must have been in '17. At that time, there were Italians building the road to Albania. How the photograph came to be there was a mystery. They showed it to the Italians and asked them about it, but nobody knew."

The photograph went the rounds again, and in the end somebody threw it into the fire. I watched it burning, and was hearing once more, in the middle of the night, between two world wars, the stifled lament of the old woman: "My Michalis! My Michalis!", and then the choking cough.

So, exactly thirty-nine years have passed between then and last summer when Triandaphyllos was here, and we counted them up. He left his Swedish wife and her son in Athens to see the Acropolis and the other sights. The two of us went off to the village. Nobody belonging to us was left there —

---

[8] During the earlier part of the First World War Greece remained neutral. In late 1916 a coup d'état led to the National Schism during which a government of National Defence was formed in Thessaloniki to assist the Allies in defending the Greek part of Macedonia against the Bulgarian invasion. The King's Government remained in Athens and in control of most of mainland Greece. The National Defence Government aided by the British navy imposed a blockade on Royalist ports, to prevent goods entering or leaving, causing shortages throughout mainland Greece apart from Macedonia; the ships of the Royalist navy were also seized. (Eds)

but you don't talk about these things. Even Triandaphyllos lowered his eyes and changed the subject, just as I was going to ask him about his relatives. As for the old woman's hut, it was now just a heap covered with grass. We stood on top of it, talking about one thing and another, jumping from Athens to Stockholm, and then to the still gaping ruins of Aryirena's residence, there in front of us. Triandaphyllos, now fifty years old, with a grey moustache, and stooped over from clearing the snow off the roads of Sweden, was poking into the piles of stones, irrepressible as ever, with his shepherd's crook from Metsovo. He had bought it in Yannena as a souvenir in a tourist shop, when we were going down Averoph Street to the port, to see Ali Pasha's castle and the mosque. He was talking and poking about doggedly, as if he had forgotten his Greek, and was searching for the words one by one in the storehouses of his memory, when, among the stones, there appeared an earthenware handle. He threw down the stick, dug with his hands, and took out a pitcher. He went mad with delight. "I'll take it to Sweden as a souvenir," he was saying rapturously. But as he turned it upside down to empty out the soil, a big, fat, short-necked toad fell out. It leapt up once, and then stayed motionless, coiled, ready to soak us with his poisonous secretions. I don't know — Triandaphyllos just said "A *ziamba*" — but my whole body froze, as if time had suddenly dissolved. Everything was whirling round in my head.

He finally took the pitcher to Sweden. A very bad idea, and he'll pay for it. Such souvenirs are like hand grenades left over from the war, buried for years among the dry leaves. Ignorant people find them now. They collect them, and the things explode suddenly, at any moment, with unforeseen consequences.

Kalamas and Acheron

> *Here is Kalamas, black Acheron he.*[1]
> Lord Byron, *Childe Harold's Pilgrimage*

At that time I was in the habit of spending the days, the months and the years on a small plateau in the fields of the monastery; at one end of the plateau, at the foot of a hill there was an old monastery, and at the other end a wreath of rocks, on the brow of the precipice. From up there you could see, on the left, the plain of Deropolis with the gleaming waters of the Drinos River, and yet further on, as far as the mountains of Aryirokastro and Tepeleni, which once groaned with cannonade at this hour, but now lay silent, washed by the rains. You could just make out the tiniest fir tree and even the vegetation which, in places,

---

[1] Kalamas is a river in Epirus (northwest Greece). It flows into the Ionian Sea. During the Axis Occupation, the left-wing resistance forces (ELAS; see note 9 on page 14) operated west of the river and the right-wing forces (EDES; see note 6 on page 11) on the east side. In the area around the Kalamas River the first battles of the Civil War took place. The Acheron or Mavropotamos (Black River) is also in northwest Greece, and also flows into the Ionian Sea, but further south than the Kalamas. According to myth the Acheron was the river of Hades, and from there souls descended to the Underworld. During the Occupation EDES operated in the region around the Acheron. The epigraph above is a retranslation of a Greek translation of words from *Childe Harold's Pilgrimage*, in which "Kalamas" had evidently been added. Byron's poem nowhere refers to Kalamas, but says only "behold black Acheron. / Once consecrated to the sepulchre. / Pluto, if this be hell I look upon . . ." (2.51). Elsewhere in his writings, Byron may have confused the two rivers; and certainly one of Byron's biographers, John Galt, makes this mistake, stating, in describing Byron's travels that "the Acheron, which they crossed in this route, is now called the Kalamas".

painted her slopes green.

The main reason I favoured this vantage point was that it was out of the way, which suited me. I didn't want to hang around, unemployed as I was, among my fellow villagers. Not that *they* were killing themselves working, of course. The best had been lost in the wars, and the most able were pining in factories in Germany, and in mines, or ploughing the plains of Australia. The few of us who remained were despondent, and the ones who tippled all day on neat ouzo wore out the greasy playing cards with their fingers, and went to the Authorities to slander one another savagely, as if all the venom had been distilled inside them. One drop, one word from them, seemingly harmless, was enough to paralyse you with the thought that it hadn't been said at random: "Idleness is the mother of all evil, teacher" — as if they knew their Ancient Greek.

Over there on the plateau, according to my mood and the hour, I would lie on the grass beneath the old walnut tree belonging to the monks, and fill the gaps in my knowledge by reading, again and again, one of my five or six books on education, or stroll about the ruined cells where wild fig trees and nettles had grown. In the mornings, I used to sit at the Kladaki, an oak tree in the saddle of the hill behind the monastery, with benches riveted to its base, hewn out of tree trunks. The pile of names carved on them, one on top of the other, were no longer legible. During the years of the Occupation, the men would gather there, the oldest that is, with Father Phousekis in the middle of them. That wasn't his name,[2] but everyone knew him by it, even the bishop of Dryïnoupolis, who, every so often, sent word to him through a villager when they went to ask him for a marriage

---

[2] "Phousekis" is a masculine form of the neuter noun *phouseki* meaning "cartridge", from Turkish *fişek*. (Eds)

certificate: "And tell that Father Phousekis that he's turning 'You have sacrificed yourselves'[3] into the *tsamiko*.[4] Who does he think he is in his old age? Father Phlesias?"[5] Once, the bishop summoned him about something to do with the monastery estates, and was making remarks to him that it wasn't right that he, as a priest . . . when Father Phousekis turned towards the glazed door of the balcony and pointed to the guerrillas who were gathered in the village square: "Do you see those men with rifles? I'll send you to the People's Court." The bishop brought the conversation back again to the monastery properties. Anyway, the men used to gather there, at Kladaki, to survey the folds of the hills to the east where our men were fighting the EDES[6] soldiers. Mortars would burst in clusters, and the machine guns would be hammering as far away as Kalamas. All the time, some villager from the auxiliary reserve would be arriving from there to change his clothes, get some bread, and go away again in the morning. And he would bring news — news that darkened the mind; that we had become worse than the Germans, that they were taking prisoners and making them dig their own graves. They would tell these things in this ambiguous way, and of course we all thought it was the others, and hated them even more. But I remember that one of these men, who had just arrived, and appeared in great

---

[3] From an anthem of the international left.
[4] A dance for young men, also popular with the *klephts* (or brigands) who fought in the Greek War of Independence (Greek Revolution). In the villages Orthodox priests are allowed to dance.
[5] A play on the name of Grigorios Papaphlesas (1788–1825), a priest and one of the instigators of the Greek Revolution of 1821. "Papa-" is from *papas* meaning "priest", hence "Father".
[6] The National Republican League (*Ethnikos Dimokratikos Ellinikos Syndesmos*), a right-wing resistance movement led by General Napoleon Zervas.

distress, was taken aside behind the sanctuary of the church by Father Phousekis who was urging him to talk.

"Come on, son — what have you to say? The EDES men, eh? It'll be Gakias."

"What Gakias, Father, and what EDES men? It's our men. May your eyes never see such a thing."

"Ours?"

They saw me, and changed the conversation. I pretended I had heard nothing, and for forty years, I didn't speak to anyone about it. But from that day, the hills undulating to the east and beyond to Kalamas looked different. That haze was not smoke from the mortars, nor was it morning mist — how can I put it? It was vapour from the Underworld. I came upon a book, an old school reader, and I read a poem by Lord Byron that was somewhat confusing:

Here is Kalamas, black Acheron he.

Things had been mixed up, so that Acheron and Kalamas became one.[7] But of course at the time I was wandering about alone in the fields of the monastery, all this was in the past. And the hills had been washed by the rains, and lay silent and harmless, like the mountains of Mourgana and Tepeleni. It was all over at last, and I was a questionable witness, uncertain even about myself — a feeling which I was experiencing for the first time in my idleness and solitude, and which followed me thereafter.

One day, a team of three workmen came to put up telegraph poles. I shut the book, and, approaching quietly, watched them working. One of them, who was wearing a dirty cap

---

[7] See the latter part of note 1 on page 9. (Eds)

with three T's[8] and a crown, started up a conversation with me. He asked who I was, and I told him. "Do you know me?" he asked. I didn't know him, but nor did he enlighten me. I braced myself to receive the next question, which I was expecting: "And what work do you do?" He leant with his hand against the telegraph pole, and appraised me thoughtfully. While the other two were gathering their tools, he hung back for a moment, and said to me, "Listen. Come to Yannena. Come next Wednesday, tomorrow week, when I'll be back there. Ask for me at the Crow Inn. Say it's for Mr Kostas. They all know *me* . . ." And at the same moment, he went off without my having time to question him further. But if a year, or two years pass by, and the discharge papers start fading in the empty wallet that Thodora, a colleague at the Zosimea Academy gave you — I wonder how she is, that soul? — with the little card, well-handled and faded too — "So you remember me always" — then necessity takes you by the hand, and leads you straight to the door of your enemy — even more so, to Gakias' door. Although, to tell the truth, I wouldn't say that I had never thought of it. But, how can I put it, I wasn't capable of such things. I wasn't "clever", as they used to tell me, and still tell me sometimes. And I was from those parts which, if you only mentioned them, made you a suspect. But I certainly couldn't deny where I came from, because one doesn't choose the place where one is born, just as one doesn't choose one's mother and father. I just tried to say it in as offhand a way as possible, without provocation.

The second question would follow: "Are you from this side, or the other side?"

"The other side," I would reply, and bow my head.

Silence would fall immediately between us, and separate

---

[8] Tachydromeia, Tilegraphia, Tilephona: Post, Telegraph, Telephone.

us, just as the Kalamas River had, at another time, separated the EDES and the ELAS[9] fighters.

This was already good enough not to dare cross Gakias' threshold. Gakias — a name that passed from mouth to mouth, but in a tone which expressed fear mixed with familiarity. They called him by his Christian name or nickname, "Gakis" or "Gakias", as they would previously have called the Bishop "Spyros from Yannena",[10] and earlier still I imagine, they would have referred to the Vizier as "Alipasas",[11] or to Skenderbey as "Skenderis".[12]

So on Wednesday, at dawn, I put on my khaki trousers that I had got in exchange, on the last day before I was discharged. The reserve second lieutenant, who looked after army supplies, was a friend of mine — what kind of friend exactly? He used to call me to the office, and I would help him. I did the accounts for him, and it seems that he was grateful, without having shown it before, however. I had never, until then, asked him for anything. I didn't want him to think that, as a foot soldier, I was going to embarrass him. I asked him only this favour, this change of clothing, so that I could have a decent pair of trousers, and step out like a human being, now that I was discharged. "These are officers' trousers," he said to me. "Act the innocent, and if the

---

[9] The National Popular Liberation Army (*Ellinikos Laïkos Apeleftherotikos Stratos*), the left-wing resistance movement led by Stephanos Saraphis.
[10] Spiridon Vlachos (1878–1954), Metropolitan of Yannena (1916–1949).
[11] The Vizier Ali Pasha (1744–1822) was of Albanian origin. As a tyrannical Pasha (governor) of Yannena and most or Epirus for forty years, he was notorious for his cunning and cruelty.
[12] George Kastriotis, or Skenderbey (1403–1486), is a national hero of Albania who had stood against the Ottoman Turks.

sergeant major passes any remark, say I gave them to you." From then on, I kept them on a wooden hanger in a nylon bag, together with a green silk shirt made from a parachute. He actually gave this to me when I had already handed in my kit, and went to say goodbye to him. I do believe that as I was leaving him, my eyes misted over, and I stumbled.

I also put on my army boots, shaved carefully, and smoothed my hair. I looked more like a commando, ready for parade, than an unemployed teacher. I went up the road to wait for the bus. Despite all the self-confidence that my smart clothes gave me, and despite all the optimism of the clear morning, there was a numbness in the depths of my heart, that spread through my body, reaching to the tips of my fingers.

During the whole ride, with its endless stops, where villagers got in and out every so often with their breadbaskets, and the bus smelt of whey, everybody kept vomiting, and I was tormenting my brain with conjectures about Mr Kostas, a person who proved to be less mysterious than I had first imagined him. When at last I met the man in question at the Crow Inn, after I had waited for hours on end in the little café, going to the door to glance out at the road every time the waiter came near me, he certainly tried to maintain his aura of mystery. He didn't show any surprise when he saw me, and scarcely said "Hello" to me, so that I thought at first that I had miscalculated this time too, and that I hadn't even managed to remember his face. He, however, without further explanation, said to me "Let's go," and made for the door. I didn't know how to begin, but finally, as we were walking side by side, I plucked up courage and asked him, "Where are we going?"

With a nod, he said flatly, "Come this way." He wasn't giving much leeway.

Then I mustered up my most polite and discreet voice, and asked him: "But how do you know me?"

He turned his head, and threw me such a haughty and absurd look that I was sure he didn't know me from Adam. And I thought how pitiful I must have been to have moved even this silly fellow, when he was questioning me that time, beside the telegraph pole. I followed. I couldn't do otherwise, and so I was led in, without a word, to the office of Gakias, formerly a captain in Zervas' army, and afterwards a permanent minister. Mr Kostas signalled to me to wait beside the entrance. He went in behind some tables where hacks were working, and bent down to the ear of this chap with a black moustache, who turned his head, looked at him furiously, or so it seemed to me, and bent over his papers again. Mr Kostas came over to me. "You wait here until they call you," he said, and left.

I waited until late in the afternoon, until the office had emptied, and black moustache had gathered his papers. Then, he raised his eyes and saw me.

"What are *you* waiting for?" he asked me. I told him my business.

"Call in tomorrow," he told me. "We're closing now."

So that was how I began to go in and out of Gakias' door, sometimes once a week, sometimes two or three times, for whole months, until there wasn't a single person who hadn't seen me, and didn't know about my case. And it was only to this chap, who was always bent over his papers, to whom it was necessary to tell everything from the beginning each time, in front of so many others also waiting their turn, until, when I had reached the end at last, he would say, "Ah yes, I remember you," only to finish off, "these days the Minister . . . Call in from Monday onwards."

"On Monday?" I would ask.

"Monday, Tuesday... come in next week, whenever suits you."

This went on until well into the autumn. The schools had been open for some time. I realised that it was now November, so I cut down on my journeys to Yannena, which cost me yet another humiliation every time, and had ruined me in fares. And then, unexpectedly, I received a note in a sealed envelope, with the Minister's name typed on the top left-hand corner. A villager had brought it to me from Yannena. He called me to the café, and as he was putting it into my hand, several pairs of eyes were raised, and looked at me venomously.

And so I found myself at the source of the River Acheron in Laka-Souli, where my bosses and underbosses enabled me to earn my bread too, if only "provisionally". And I should be "proud", said the Minister's note, because I would be "offering my services to this heroic region where General Napoleon Zervas..." and so on. But it seems that I was exceptionally lucky, because the house of the chairman of the local council, where I was to stay, had been the General's Headquarters, as the chairman informed me, almost as soon as I crossed his threshold, having endured the country road with its endless corners and hills, and the rain pouring down my face, because the car had left me somewhere half an hour away. The chairman was a fine-looking, good-hearted man, tall and strongly built, with a grey, upturned moustache. He took my jacket, and put it on a chair in front of the fire to dry, while his wife brought in a tray with raki.[13] "The world

---

[13] *Raki* is term applied to a variety of highly alcoholic drinks distilled from grape, often flavoured with aniseed. Similar to *ouzo* but ouzo may be made from alcohol from any source.

and his uncle have dried out here, teacher," he told me. "All the soaking wet people in Laka. Zervas used to sit at this fireside, there, where you're sitting. He had some backside, I can tell you. Two stools wouldn't hold it. Zervas there, and Gakias opposite."

And afterwards, when he was climbing the creaking wooden staircase with an oil lamp in his hand to show me to my room, he sighed: "Ah son, you'll be sleeping in the General's bed. Aren't you the lucky one!"

I was so dazed by the journey, that everything seemed like a strange fairy tale. But when I awoke in the morning and looked around the room, I didn't see anything left there to be overawed by. There was a table and two chairs in the middle, a chest with bedding piled on it between the two windows, and above me the beams without a ceiling. It was only when I got up that I saw on the wall, above my pillow, a large photograph of Zervas, the one with the black forage cap and the beard. I went out onto the balcony, where the sink was, and washed. Then I stood in front of the window, and gazed at the mist coming down from a veiled Olytsika, stepping over the saddle of the Variades mountains, and spreading in the dark valley with its muddy river, the Acheron. The mountains of Souli were lost in the clouds. It was cold, and still drizzling.

Then the chairman came in with the coffee and glasses of raki: "What are you staring at, teacher? Nothing but hilltops. Sit down and drink the coffee with me. It's still early."

We sat at the table facing each other, and he came straight to the point: "By the way, teacher, we got into conversation about other things yesterday, and I didn't ask you where you come from."

There was a short silence. I looked at the photograph opposite, and saw Zervas himself, looking at me askance.

"From the Kalamas region," I said.

"This side or the other?"

"The other."

Dismayed, he said, "Oh poor lad, oh son!" and bent over the tray. He took one of the glasses of raki, and put it in front of me.

"Ah well, here's to us," he sighed, "and to a good winter."

"A good winter," I said, and involuntarily my eyes took in the bare room, the draughty windows, the roof gaping above me without a ceiling. I was already shivering with cold. What would it be like when winter really came on?

The chairman drew his cup of coffee towards him, and sipped at it noisily. Then, leaning over the table, he said confidentially, "Listen to me. The things our eyes have seen can't be forgotten. We became worse than the Germans. Do you hear, they made prisoners dig their own graves!"

My mind darkened. The years became a hopeless tangle inside me. I lowered my eyes.

"Our men?" I whispered.

"Ours. The EDES men," said the chairman. "Ten years have passed, and I haven't told anyone else."

I pulled myself together. I hope the man is well, if he is still alive. Without him, how could I have got through that winter?

Another thirty years have passed since then. In all that time, I have wondered how on earth do you talk to people, how do you communicate with others when — yes, all right, you use more or less the same language as everyone else, but each of us has other things on our mind when we speak. And if you talk about Acheron, they think you mean Pluto and Persephone, and the narcissus she plucked one spring in the meadow of death, and other such myths they have supposedly been filled with during their childhood. They imagine that, as a teacher, you have a purpose in life — the one and only — to set them down once more at the desk, and make their heads dizzy lecturing them. Nor are you talking about the Acheron which tourists cross today when they travel on the Corfu-to-Athens coach, somewhere on the Phanari plain, once the plain of Acherousia, and in the drowsiness and tedium of midday, with eyes that have wandered aimlessly around nudist beaches and other seaside places on the island, they gaze at the gorge where the mythical river of the dead emerges.

You see. You are talking about the other side, the invisible side. As if we were saying — the other side of death.

The hoopoe

This time, he went down very early to the sea, just before dawn. He was always awakened at the same time by the vague anxiety that worked on him like an alarm clock. He jumped out of bed, and grabbed the clock to confirm, yet again, that it was too early to start his day — a summer day that would drag, without the office. But it was too late to go back to sleep again. He slipped out as quietly as possible, so as not to disturb his landlord and landlady, who, he already suspected, didn't look too kindly on him. He had never been able to have a conversation with them.

On the beach, he found only a few fishermen who must have taken up position there since dark, with their folding stools and baskets of implements beside them. He sat away from them, and gazed at the sea that lay stretched out in front of him, and was then filled with iridescent light, as the sun emerged behind it out of a mist that threatened a burning hot day. Really, when he came to think about it, he should be content. He had finally succeeded in getting himself a permanent job in the Civil Service — in "getting hold of the brass ring", as Vangelis would say, who used to break out in a cold sweat, and soak his pillow when he saw the years passing, and his brother still unemployed, with the school leaving certificate in his pocket, and no security. Yet Vangelis' past, above all, "gave no guarantees whatsoever".

TITLE. The Eurasian hoopoe (*Upupa epops*) is a migratory bird of striking appearance with its long beak, large crest and high-pitched call (which the name *hoopoe* evokes). Its distinctive looks and call have given it symbolic significance in many cultural traditions.

Nor was he one of those wide-boys with dark glasses, flowery tie, and leather briefcase in his hand, who can manage on nothing. And then there was his sickly constitution, that had been weakened even further by the deprivations and illnesses of the Occupation, when the Germans were hunting them, and they moved from thicket to thicket, and drank stagnant water, with long-legged insects floating on the green surface. In the end, he was saved by an English doctor whom Vangelis brought down from the mountains. Then came the parcels from UNRA.[2] With the soups and tinned food, Allied help got into his bloodstream.

So, it was good that he had found this job. The salary was low, of course, and the boss was stupid, but bosses in the Civil Service always have to be stupid. A clever man is not reduced to ending his life as a boss in the Civil Service. And had he forgotten the stairs he went up and down, with that knot in his stomach, like a fist, and a bitter taste of quinine in his mouth? And the doors his family had knocked on? And Vangelis, the older brother, who gave his youth to the struggle for "justice and freedom", only to waste away in bed, his insides done for. For fifteen years, he dragged him to the ground-floor apartments of Athens, to Anthoupolis, Petroupolis, Ayios Yerotheos, and for fifteen years, Vangelis was homesick for their birthplace. When he had no hope left, his yearning was like a permanent yearning for death.

He was finally at peace last summer, and they brought him to the village. They arrived at midnight, worn out with his last hours and the long journey — five people in the car, and the body in a coffin strapped to the boot. The house that they had repaired as well as they could after the fire, the house that had sheltered them for a few more years, and that they tried to maintain from a distance, writing to this one

[2] United Nations Relief Agency.

and begging that one, had finally been eaten away forever by time and neglect. But it was still standing, to fulfil this purpose as well — the last, to all appearances. His family sat up all night around the coffin. He took charge of the sick-bed clothes, which had been wrapped in an old blanket, to be burned. In Athens, at times like these, it was not easy to do this job. Throwing them into the street — as a relative suggested — was an idea that incensed the women. In the middle of the night, he went to the ravine. There was a cave there that he suddenly remembered, but in the dark, it was difficult to find the path. However, his feet soon found the familiar footprints all by themselves. He pushed the bundle into the opening, bathed it in alcohol that had been used for massaging the patient, threw the kindling on it and moved away. He sat on a large stone. The flames filled the hollow, overflowed, and licked the rock, scattering fierce tongues of fire, and consuming anything that remained. Then they drew together, shrank down — and it was dark again. The clear sound of water rose from the stream below. Above his head, the stars trembled with a cool light, and a wind came up that murmured first in the foliage, and then passed lightly by him, caressing his thinning hair. His nerves relaxed, and he began to moan softly, until he fell asleep like a child, with his head on his knees.

It was nearly dawn when he was wakened by the cold. At first, he didn't notice anything, then he heard a mournful cry, something between the screech of an owl and the squeal of a bat. He shivered. "It's the souls of the dead." "It isn't the souls of the dead, it's the hoopoe." Then everything became clear around him. The stars shone here and there on a background that was beginning to whiten, and the cry of the hoopoe was rising now from the ravine, together with the sound of the water invisibly flowing. It was dawning, and he had to go back to the house, where the others were sitting up.

So then, Vangelis was at rest, and at last, for the first time, he too could have a holiday — fifteen whole days on an Aegean island.

His mistake was that he hadn't looked about early enough for company. Rather, he left it almost to the day before his departure. Lena was out of the question, of course — an intelligent girl, graceful as a deer, with a ready wit. All the time, it was "Miss Lena, somebody wants to see you," and murmured conversations on the phone until, one day, the Head of Department couldn't put up with it anymore. "Miss Lena, you make a lot of telephone calls." She put him in his place once and for all. "Please charge them to me, sir. One would pay any money for some things, don't you think?" Teta might have agreed to come with him, if she hadn't booked to go abroad with a group — to Yugoslavia, Austria, and returning via Italy. The way he had managed things, there was nothing left for him but the sea. As if to put an end to these thoughts, he undressed, and walked a little way into the shallows, caressing his body that was scorched by the sun, and fell into the cool water. When he came out onto the sand again, the sun had risen, and was becoming hot. Parties of people began to invade the beach, and the meltemi started up.³ Until the afternoon, the place would be boiling. He didn't stay any longer.

He called in at the little tavern to get something to eat. It was full of young people, boys with girls in bikinis lounging on plastic chairs beneath the climbing vine. Their own vine was

---

³ The meltemi is a summer wind in the Aegean which blows from the north in the daytime. (Eds)

bigger, but it had been scorched when the Germans burned the house. One spring, Vangelis had taken the saw and cut off the dead branches. That shit of a gypsy was passing by at the time and told them about the atomic bomb that the Americans had exploded on Bikini Atoll.[4] His face lit up, and he couldn't stop talking about it, until Vangelis cut him short. "What do you think of the vine? Will it give us any fruit again?" He went off, almost dancing, and he sang:

> *for uncle Truman with the bomb*
> *will trim their red wings[5] back . . .*

"A bad dog never dies," said Vangelis, cutting away the dead wood. In the end, the vine didn't thrive. They took Vangelis, and he struggled to survive in barren island after barren island.[6] His strength went from him bit by bit in that hellish terrain, and in the interrogation rooms.

At the tavern counter, two lanky Germans, beanpods with manes, were standing, drinking beer. He took a mortadella, cheese and tomato sandwich, and as he was paying for it, he murmured to the tavern owner, "A bad dog never dies." Maybe he didn't hear the remark, absorbed as he was in his work. Or perhaps the world had changed in the meantime, and he hadn't noticed it. He cast a final, bitter glance at the Germans, and headed morosely for his room,

[4] The first atomic tests at Bikini Atoll took place in July 1946. There were no further tests until 1 March 1954, when a new more powerful type of bomb was used. The reference to "spring" might suggest 1954, but by then Truman was no longer US president, and, from what follows, it appears that this was happening before Vangelis' imprisonment during the Greek Civil War. This is most probably, then, late news from July 1946, the encounter taking place in the spring of 1947. (Eds)

[5] "Red" meaning communist; the reference is to the Soviet Union. (Eds)

[6] Leftists were imprisoned in camps on the islands of Yaros, Limnos, Ayios Stratis and Makronisos before, during and after the Civil War of 1946–1949.

eating on the way.

When he came into the paved yard of the house, he looked at the wall, beside the honeysuckle. The cage was still there, and the hoopoe shook the little fan on its crest with the white spots, tilted its head, and looked sideways at him. In the corridor, he could hear people talking in the room next to his, and he stopped short. His landlord and landlady were eating inside. He heard the noise of cutlery, as well as remarks from mouths filled with food. The woman was saying, "What's all this fuss about the hoopoe? Would you believe it? He says he can't listen to it screaming from five in the morning." And the man said, "Take the cage off the wall, and hang it in the lemon tree out of the way . . . until the week's over and he's gone . . ." Was it a coincidence, or did they hear him coming? He tiptoed into his room, locked the door, and threw himself onto the wrought-iron bed. From here, nothing could be heard except the meltemi, which he could feel banging against the burning walls. The shutter didn't close properly. A reflection from the sun came in, hitting the wall next to it, and then striking him. It was hot.

"It's hot," said their mother, and she wiped her face with her apron. Her movement could only be sensed, because the room was in darkness. If there had been any light, they would have seen the round, wide-open eyes of the little girl who kept on asking, "What are they doing now? Why are they banging on the doors?" "They're not banging on the doors," their mother said quietly, to calm her down for fear she would start crying. "They have the mules loaded, and the tins are rattling." And they did have loaded mules. Through the trampling of the soldiers, you could hear their hooves slipping on the big stones. But the loud bangs must have been doors breaking, because at the same time, you could hear women screaming and children wailing. "Why are they doing that now? Why are they shouting?" the little one was asking. And he whispered in her ear, "They're not shouting. They're speaking German. The wind's blowing outside. That's why you think they're shouting." There was no wind blowing. The August heat was stifling. When the trampling feet had gone away, their door suddenly opened. Their mother jumped up, and the man who entered covered the child's mouth with his palm. "Don't be frightened," Vangelis said. "It's me." Their mother cried out in despair, "Why did you come? They'll catch you. They're still passing through." What followed happened so quickly. He remembered, only confusedly, that they went out the back gate into the vineyard, going along, bent over, from fence to fence — that a thorn caught him on the bare arm, and gave him a fright — that they could hear strange voices on the road, and Vangelis shoved him into the ditch. Then, he gave the child to their mother, and unslung his rifle. He placed it on the bank, pointing it towards the road. But the voices moved away. At one point, Vangelis whispered, "The house is on fire," and they sat up to see. It wasn't only their own house that was on fire. All the houses were in flames. The place was glowing. Cries could be heard, then gunshots, and the cries ceased. But one cry persisted, a cry that came from the depths, as if from another world. "What's he saying?" "It'll be old Manthos. They'll have trapped him in his hut." "He's stopped now. The smoke'll have smothered him." The hut could be seen, still standing there, at the end of the village, below our house. Then the flames enveloped it. No more cries were heard, only one of the last roofs collapsing noisily, and the flames roaring. Then only the flames. "It's hot," said Vangelis, and wiped his face with his right hand, his left still holding the rifle. Towards dawn, it got a little cooler. Then, a wailing cry was heard from the opposite hedge, and again farther away in the fields. "It's the souls of those who were killed." "It isn't those who were killed. It's a hoopoe."

"It's a hoopoe, a *hoo-poe*," his landlady was explaining down in the yard. Heavy footsteps beat on the paving. "Let me show you your room. The one next to it will be empty in a few days." He could hear the footsteps now in the corridor, as well as the woman's voice. "It's an island room. How do you call it? *Couleur locale*." "*Ja, ja*," the Germans were saying, and the woman was cackling with laughter, while the meltemi howled on the walls that *they* had set fire to. He remembered, and was lonely, as all those who remember are lonely.

Big Mother

For Spyros

Her memorial service takes place today, the twentieth of December. A year has passed. I would very much like to be there, but reasons stronger than my will prevent me. A month ago, we booked for our Christmas holidays at a hotel in Delphi, where my daughter, who is quite grown up now, will have the opportunity to go up to the ski resort on Parnassos, all ready to spread her wings and fly. She often practises yodelling, and has bought all her equipment: alpine cap and pullover, woollen scarf with fringe, ski suit and anorak, special boots, and of course, skis and ski poles. All this cost a fortune. My Christmas bonus hardly covered it. My salary will have to pay for the other expenses: the hotel, and meals at the self-service in the ski club, and in the evening at Karathanasis' tavern in Arachova, where the other skiers from Athens will be gathering in their ski suits, their faces flushed with fresh air. *I* think it's all fantasy on my daughter's part, but to be fair, there really is no way I can turn her against fantasies she isn't responsible for creating.

Last year, it was different; because of the whole psychological atmosphere that was created by the long-distance telephone call, and the sudden announcement of the event, there was no time for reflection. Whatever way you look at it, a death that you are told about on the telephone is more compelling than a death notice stuck on the pillar of the Electricity Service Building, or at the corner of the street, along with election posters. It's even more compelling than the ambulance siren that, every so often, sweeps down Alexandras Avenue, and is then lost in the roar of the other cars, rushing behind it into the void.

It would appear that the name Big Mother also played a part, with God knows what resonance, especially as connections with my family tree are vague and hazy, if not completely blurred.

The truth is that Big Mother was not a close relative. Apart from ourselves, who certainly had special reasons for doing so, everyone called her that in our village, where she ruled over us with her height and her shadow, as well as with her family — in-laws, children, and grandchildren — and their old-fashioned house beside ours. A house that the centuries respected, and, I could almost say, the Germans too — but not *our* house. Because *they* certainly didn't respect anything, and if Big Mother's house escaped their cleansing fire, it is because the floor was beaten earth, and the small windows were like embrasures. So the kindling they gathered in the back rooms, two bundles of dried grass from the barns, was incapable of setting fire to the thick beams made of whole tree trunks, that had been well cured with smoke. The lighted kindling suffocated on the smoke, and went out. By the way, I would like to make it clear that they *did* burn our homes with kindling; what they said about dust that caught fire from a pistol shot was a fantasy of the villagers, who couldn't explain how the Germans had time to light so many fires, which were surely caused by excessive zeal.

Well then, I took advantage of the confusion that prevailed immediately after the phone call, to avoid second thoughts — I would be driving five hundred kilometres, in winter weather, and the forecast said there would be snow — I put on my heavy jacket and astrakhan fur cap, that I had bought the year before last during similar weather, in a tourist shop in Portaria, and hit the road in my nine horsepower Datsun, feeling rather like a noble Russian setting off on his troika for the boundless steppes.

The truth is that the weather aided such fantasies, because from Makrynoros and beyond, the slopes were all white. It was still snowing up on the hills, and looked as if it would be coming down to the low ground. It got dark early, and soon I was driving on a road lightly covered with snow, without traffic, the snowflakes whirling in front of the headlights. I passed villages muffled in snow, with lighted windows, behind which I could imagine people chatting around the stove, and children turning somersaults on their beds before going to sleep.

On the Yannena plateau, where I arrived near midnight, the snow had frozen on the roads. All traffic had stopped, and I was almost skidding, leaning forward on the steering wheel, with my face stuck to the clouded windscreen, until I arrived at the entrance to the town, and stopped at the first hotel.

There were few guests in the lounge. The tourists hadn't arrived yet for Christmas, with their woollen caps and boots. However, the Christmas tree had taken its place in a corner, and the coloured lights were going on and off by themselves; they were rehearsing. Five or six men, like those one sees on weekdays in hotels — shopkeepers and salesmen — were killing time watching television. But I was tired after my difficult journey. I went straight up to my room, and ordered tea.

I am often slow in getting to sleep when I'm tired. I lay on top of the blankets, and confused images went round and round in my head — mostly of the person I was going to say goodbye to. I could see her, bent over, but huge, climbing the stone stairway, and then turning her wrinkled face, half-covered with her headscarf, and shouting to me, "Will you come when I die?" She had always been hard of hearing, even in her youth. This made her shout loudly, as if it were others who couldn't hear. In the old days, the plain, the winter grazing lands and the village would resound when she scolded her husband, old Zikos, after he'd come back from the café smelling of tobacco. He would smoke secretly in the café, where they would give him cigarettes — more for their own amusement, because very soon afterwards, they would hear her shouting at him. Other old stray memories wandered about in my head. A big, low, round table in the middle of the house, with bent, silent heads all around, bending forward to eat from a shallow copper bowl — old men, younger men, women and children, who I didn't recognise bent over like that. I could hear only their lips smacking, and the spoons tapping. A wooden kneading trough in the corner, filled with the precious cornflour, and Big Mother with the wooden spoon stirring it with one hand, and pouring boiling water into it with the other. Her bread that we ate. Women with flushed faces, baking at the oven. Babies without trousers, crawling on all fours on the ground. Sheep bleating at the foot of the mountain, just where the lower slopes end, and the plain begins — on Zikos' winter grazing land. And in the night, a fire lit in the ditch of the big cornfield, near the river, and beside it mattresses in a row, with faces outside the blankets, counting the stars. Wild boar snaffling the corn, and the dogs barking. And then those beanpoles, the Germans, half-naked, with dog-tags hanging on their breasts — and in the night, fires and machine guns, until I fell asleep.

In the morning, when I got up to continue my journey, it wasn't snowing anymore, but the sky was overcast, and the town was still muffled up. I phoned the traffic police. The road to Pogonia was passable, but only if you had chains. It wasn't a problem, because the equipment in my car is complete, from rev counters and chains, to sun visors and a little doll hanging from the mirror. I passed through snowy valleys that knew me, and I knew them — inside out — through oak forests, where, perhaps, there were still wolves and wild boar, if they hadn't gone down from the snowy weather to Zikos' winter grazing below. What winter grazing, what wolves, and what wild boar? Looking ahead of me at Mourgana, the terrible mountain with the dark name, burdened with snow and clouds, I arrived at the village. I cast a furtive glance at my ruined home, and went straight to the gate next door.

In the middle of the house was the open coffin, the waxen face half-covered with the headscarf, and in her folded hands, the old icon of Saint Basil that we used to carry around the houses on New Year's Eve. I took off my hat, and bowed my head. Five or six old men, her neighbours, were sitting all round on stools. Old Zikos was sitting cross-legged on the low wooden bed, beside the fire that was burning brightly. His thick moustache drooped. I bent down and kissed him. "You came," he said to me, and lowered his eyes to the fire. And then, "It was her time." That's all he said.

I sat on a stool opposite him. He asked me about my family, how my journey had been. "I shouldn't have told them to telephone you, to put you to such trouble . . . And how are things in Athens with the new government?" He offered to make me coffee, and showed the woman, who got up, where the coffee pot and coffee jar were, and the bottle of raki. Then, he arranged some coals himself, with the tongs, and told the woman the amounts — so much coffee, so much sugar. I remembered that he had always made the coffee himself. At that time, I was among the last remaining villagers. Indeed, for two years, when I was discharged from the army, and until I found work, I was always calling in with them, winter and summer. My family had already scattered to the four winds. Opposite the village, Mourgana was still smoking from the war. Everything happened in those years. I spent lonely days and months wandering about, usually with an old double-barrelled gun, in wild places and fallow fields, mostly gaping at the ravens flapping unsteadily in the wind. I was being soaked by a dampness that would kill you — poverty, loneliness, and the uncertain future. I avoided going to the café with the regular customers, where the owner, a bastard, thought nothing of telling you bluntly to clear out of the corner if you were sitting without drinking his tepid ouzo. Sometimes I would listen to the news on the radio, always silently and without comment, because every Monday, he would go off early in the morning, two hours on foot, and report whatever we had said to the stationmaster — word for word. Then, I would discreetly draw old Zikos away, and we would go to his house. We used to sit at the fire and chat. He would make coffee, and I would explain the news to him, and read him the newspaper, if one had come down from Yannena. He would listen, and shake his head.

So now I had become one of the family again, just as before, when they had given me hospitality during even worse times.

"Yannis?" I asked him.

"In Australia."

"Mitros?"

"In Belgium first — now Germany."

"Tolis?"

"In Germany too."

"And Kollias?"

"You're asking *me* about Kollias? And you come from

Athens."

"The snow'll have cut him off. He wouldn't have been able to get here in time. He probably has no chains," I said.

"That'll be it . . ." he said. And then, "Have a cigarette." I thought about the dead woman, Big Mother, and her abhorrence of cigarettes, but I didn't say anything. The old man, still sitting cross-legged, was smoking thoughtfully, moustache drooping, eyes fixed on the flames. And when they came shortly afterwards to take away the coffin, and the priest came in dressed in his stole, stamping his feet to shake off the snow, and four men with him — I didn't know them, he must have picked them up somewhere else — the old man just said, "My dearest."

I stayed to keep him company, until the others returned. On the table where the coffin had been, there remained an earthenware dish with bread, a large wax candle — the flame serenely rising — and a rusty censer that filled the house with the perfume of incense. And the old man, sitting cross-legged, smoking his second cigarette.

Koriandolino

For I. Ch. Papadimitrakopoulos

Here it is again — May Day, and it has fallen on a Tuesday. That means four whole days' holiday, including the Monday in between, because some people have officially, and others unofficially, taken this day off as well — in the end everyone is enjoying the benefit of it — and Athens has emptied. Which is all to the good. It is a thousand times better here than running to the country resorts and the suburbs — what country resorts and what suburbs? — for the waiters to keep you sitting for hours in front of a paper tablecloth, with a little basket of stale bread, and for them to stretch your nerves to breaking point, for you to loathe them, and May Day, and yourself, and then to drive back in the endless traffic jams — start, stop, start, stop — "No, you should have taken the middle lane." "No, it's your fault for not helping" — until you're at loggerheads with your wife and child.

For the first time, it's so quiet in here without that incessant din, that every so often reaches a climax when the buses accelerate to get up the hill. Last year, at a similar time, when May Day fell within the Easter holiday, we decided to go to Rhodes — we're only human after all. Life is short — one never knows what is going to happen. We can't leave the world without having set foot on the Greek Honolulu, a couple of steps from our door, even though we did hear that song all through our youth — how did it go?

> *The wild wave tells me I should kiss you*
> *sweetheart of mine in Honoluloo-oo-oo.*

We learned to sing it in Yannena, poor victims of the *andartes*[1] that we were, from the loudspeaker in front of the Titania cinema, with the calligraphic neon sign — the letters giving out an orange light that flickered, magically. And the rain never stopped dripping from the crooked umbrellas, soaking our shoes, with their unstitched uppers.

So, we decided to go to Rhodes for Easter, despite the fact that it's really more of a summer place. That's the time when remote coasts and other beaches fill up with Scandinavian girls, stark-naked, with a ball of black hair between their thighs — even though their heads are blond. How is it that they have so much hair? It's enough to addle your brain! But how could you go in the summer? Where would you stay? What would you eat? Everything is so expensive. You couldn't eye up the girls, when your wife and little daughter are with you. What would they think of you afterwards, and how could you bear to look them in the eye?

It's ten o'clock, and they're still sleeping. They've had their fill of sleep — the budding season has got hold of them, it seems. Opposite my table, the balcony door is open, and the sun is falling on my geraniums. Although mangy with dust and fumes, their scarlet flowers are radiant. On the sideboard, the bottle of Koriandolino that we bought in Rhodes, and still haven't opened, is shining too. It's an orange liqueur, with twigs in it made of crystallized sugar, that bring to mind icicles hanging on trees, and from the eaves of houses, when the snow freezes at night. We hadn't any heating in our house — it's funny to think of it — only the fire in the kitchen. When we went to our rooms afterwards, they were freezing, so we would slip under the thick, heavy blankets, and pull them up until they covered our heads. In the morning, the condensation would have

---

[1] Guerrilla soldiers, or partisans, who fought in the resistance movements.

frozen the panes of the balcony door, forming strange forests, with broad-leafed trees, wings, and cataracts that became iridescent in the morning sun — all the dreams of the night. When you breathed on the pane from inside, that world was lost in tears. You wiped it then with your palm, and the village appeared, covered in snow, with sparse footprints on the paths, icicles on the eaves and, in the garden, the curly lettuce protruding here and there, above the snow. A blackbird would hop about, pecking at the tender shoots of lettuce. He visited our garden every time there was snow. A little timid, yet cheeky too — he was almost comical. You could sit and gaze at him for hours. Until one morning, in the winter of '40, Thodorelos killed him from the window with his Mannlicher. The whole house reverberated with the shot. We went outside, and saw the blackbird lying motionless, with no head, beside a red stain, its wings spread out in the snow.

That winter, a mountain battery camped in the village, from the end of November '40, until the middle of March '41. How it came to be there, when there was so much heavy gunfire from behind Nemertsika, and as far as Aryirokastro, especially at night, is one of those strange things that sometimes happens. It was as if they had muddled up the papers at Staff Quarters — which wouldn't be at all improbable — and they had forgotten the battery. In any case, for three months, our village became a camp. The roads were full of foot soldiers who would chat away together on the yard walls. There were bugle calls in the morning for breakfast, and at midday for the mess that they set up in the middle of the village, and in the evening for taps. But the sweetest was the reveille, the French one, that the bugle played at daybreak, when it was still dark.

The soldiers stayed in the houses, which were

commandeered. Our own house was large, two-storied — we had just moved into it when I was born. It had ceilings, a balcony, and an inner wooden staircase with a bannister that I used to slide down to reach the bottom more quickly. So then, in our house, they commandeered the upper rooms, and the captain, one Yoannis Sarris from Athens, installed himself. He was a short, fat little man with red cheeks. He also had his batmen with him — two soldiers, natives of Old Greece, Vasilis Thodorelos from Lechena in the Ileia district, and Nikos Gadzioris from Astros in Kynouria. At first, my father was far from happy about it. We had sisters, and he would glare at the two soldiers, especially at Thodorelos, whose left eye was smaller than the other. My father thought he was winking at my sister out of badness — "Old Greeks, dirty Morean[2] dogs." But Thodorelos, who had a heart of gold, knew nothing about such things, and would be in and out of our kitchen, sometimes to ask for plates to cover the captain's soup when it came to the boil, sometimes for a spice for his food — he had him spoiled. He would bring us rough tallow candles, so that the women could knit. The winter evenings fell early, and it was pitch-black. They would come, after putting their darling to bed, and settle down on the stools. You couldn't get them out of the house. But they would sit well back, especially Gadzioris, who was timid, and blushed whenever my mother said to him, "Come on, you, up to the fire, Nikos, and warm yourself. Don't be shy."

Then Thodorelos would prattle endlessly about the land he owned at Lechena. We should see *real* ploughing, where the ploughshare can produce huge yields, not like our poor soil. And they didn't send their women out to work in the

---

[2] Greeks from the Morea, another name (of medieval origin) for the Peloponnese.

fields — not like they do here — he wanted to say. We were looking at a man who had two horses, one for the plough and cart, the other for racing. We should see that horse. It stood higher than the captain's.

Sarris's strawberry roan was indeed magnificent. It was slender, and its coat shone. They combed it every morning. Then Thodorelos would mount it, and ride through the narrow streets like lightning from one end to the other, and then across the village, dismounting in our yard. The horse would neigh happily, and champ, frothing at the bit. When our father wasn't around, my eldest sister would laugh, and say to him, "You've worn out that horse, Vasilis. God help you if the captain sees what you're up to." And he would say, "To hell with the captain. What does he know about riding?" And his left eye would get smaller. I became brave too. He would lift me up behind him on the saddle. My arms weren't long enough to go right round his waist, so I would grab hold of the broad leather belt that he wore over his jacket. And as he spurred the horse and dashed forward, I could see, between half-closed eyes, the hedges and trees flying by, and the hollow feeling in my stomach went right through my body. In the evening, beside the fire, Thodorelos would say to me, "When the war's over, all being well, you'll see the races we'll have on the plain, as far as the eye can see, not like here, in the streets." Stupefied by the fire, I would gaze at him like an idiot, open-mouthed. Gadzioris would sit away from us, with his back against the grain tub, and rarely speak. "What about *you*, Nikos?" my mother would ask. "Have *you* any land?" "We have. We have some," he would reply. And Thodorelos would shake his head as if to say, "Leave those ones alone. They're not talkers."

Kostas Alexopoulos was the last to join us. He owned the "Picadilly" in Athens, so they said. It was "the biggest café-confectioner in the Balkans", according to Thodorelos. Alexopoulos was quietly spoken, and was always rubbing his hands. He never got angry, even when Thodorelos would say to him, "You Athenian bums". He stayed next door at the widow Yotena's house, with Pavlakos. Every week, he received parcels through the post — big boxes — and then they would gather in our yard, the whole lot of them, with Pavlakos too, and the one with the small beard, the mysterious Stamoulis. They would eat the cakes together. Now that I remember, it's occurred to me that, among the parcels, there must have been that bottle of the captain's with the Koriandolino.

We rarely went up to the upper floor of the house — especially never when the captain was in his room. We would hear him calling "Tho'relos," and then the quick footsteps of Vasilis and his voice, "Sir."

One evening, Thodorelos came down looking very cross, and asked us for some camomile. "What does he want now?" asked Nikos, who had come down earlier to get hot water for compresses. "He wants me to rub him down with cologne, if you please. He can go to hell. *I'm* not acting the nurse for him." Gadzioris blushed, and turned his head sideways, as he always did. That evening, there was a great fuss on the floor above. The captain had to get up at dawn, to go to Kakavia, where the officers were having a meeting. And as if that wasn't enough, he had caught a bad cold. He had a fever. He couldn't touch food, and he had a pain in his stomach. All the time, we were hearing shouts and "Sir", and footsteps back and forth above our heads.

In the morning, there was calm. I went up to get a saucepan that my mother needed. Nikos went into the captain's room, and left the door open. I was hit by a strong smell of stale air, and eau-de-Cologne — the stuffiness of the sick room. Nikos was taking his time. I looked in. I saw him opening the window, and then he bent over a wooden army trunk. And I saw, on the captain's little table, that bottle, the orange one, that had whole twigs made of crystallized sugar inside it. When Nikos gave me the saucepan, it was filled with raisins. He said, "Give them to your sisters," but I just gaped at him. I was at a loss for words.

That day, when the captain was away, we stuffed ourselves with figs and raisins, but my mind was still on that marvel that my eyes had seen. A strange calm prevailed, as if everyone were walking on tip-toe. The soldiers were gathering at the crossroads, and chatting among themselves. Our own soldiers kept disappearing. And when the bugle blew in the afternoon for roll call, it sounded strange — somehow hollow. The next day, at dawn, the battery left for the front.

We put up our beds again in the empty rooms.

During the time that followed, up until the middle of April, life became difficult. With the army gone, the village was suddenly deserted, and in the middle of the calm, the cannons could be heard loudly now, even during the day. And when the spring and good weather had settled in, the aeroplanes appeared as well. They meandered about in the sky above our village, from one mountain ridge to the other. These were reconnaissance planes. We weren't afraid of them. But then they started diving, and disappearing into the ravines. You could hear their machine guns. They would go straight up into the sky. We knew from their vertical diving that they were Stukas. The retreat had begun. The soldiers who had come back from the front stayed hidden in their dug-outs all day. They built their foxholes with dry stones — later, we found abandoned helmets, cartridge pouches, army blankets, water bottles, mess-tins, even spools of thread and needles. People had to make do during the Occupation. Only when night fell, did they put their heads out. They would walk through the village street in rags, their boots falling to pieces, their leggings dragging in the mud, their eyes fierce. They were ready for a fight. They knocked on the doors asking for bread. We gave them whatever we had. What had *we*? "What's left for us?" we would say to them.

At last, one evening, the mountain battery passed through. What mountain battery? Only a few remnants. We hardly recognized Thodorelos. He was unshaven, muddy, and limping, with a wound in his forehead where the blood had dried. We took him inside, and washed him. My mother chased my oldest sister away. She sent her to my aunt's, on the pretext that she had to go and grind wheat with the hand mill. She went off sulking. We asked Thodorelos about the others, and where Nikos was. His eyes filled with tears, and he shook his head. *Nikos had gone.* Then we gave him clean clothes belonging to my father. My mother took his own clothes that were full of lice, doused them in petrol behind the yard wall, and set fire to them. She carried them out with a rake. We set him down to eat. We had some chickpeas. Then he told us how it happened. "The captain was to blame for it all," he said. "The Italians had spotted us, and he was giving the command for us to attack, when the major himself, Sengounas, came down the hill and grabbed him by the collar. 'I'll shoot you, captain,' he shouted. 'You shouldn't even be a corporal.' He caused their deaths." Thodorelos left the same evening, with the others.

During all this time, my youngest sister had disappeared. My mother was searching everywhere for her, and she found her in the room above, in the dark. "You're *here* and I've been looking for you all this time," she said quietly to her.

"Come down and we'll eat some bread. They've gone."
"Leave me alone. I'm not hungry. I'm going to bed," she replied.

In the morning, we heard that Charikleia, Yotena's daughter, was missing from our neighborhood. Pavlakos had put an army greatcoat on her, and a forage cap, and had taken her with him. They made up a song about it:

> *My Pavlakos, my Pavlakos,*
> *take me to the barracks*
> *so I can polish up your buttons*
> *and the golden crown.*

They could say what they liked. She ended up in Athens — married.

As for us — in the end it's each to his own fate, as they say. But those were very difficult years. A whirlwind that turned everything upside-down. What can we say about it? And yet in the midst of all these tempests, I carried the memory of that bottle of the captain's, with the icicles in it. Like refugees, who, when they have lost everything, come to rest somewhere with a thimble on their breast, that they kept, no matter what, without realising it. In all this time, I've often asked about the name of that drink, but nobody understood what I meant. Just once, someone said to me, "Ah, I know which one you mean, but I don't know what it's called." Until last year, during the Easter holidays, which we spent in Rhodes. I was gazing into the shop windows, in the old town, and I saw it among bottles of whisky, Benedictine and Tia Maria. I asked in the shop, and they told me that it is called *Koriandolino*. "Ah, that's what you meant," my wife said to me. "Why do you want it? It isn't up to much." And my daughter said, "Papa, you're always buying old-fashioned things."

My childhood friend, Ismail Kadare

It turns out that the Albanian writer Ismail Kadare, from Aryirokastro in the Deropolis district — whose book *The General of the Army of the Dead*[1] came to us by registered post from Paris — is an old friend, from the time we were children of about the same age, and without our ever having met each other. Yet we are friends, in that special, very profound manner of children, who, when they meet for the first time, look at each other thoughtfully, and then suggest very seriously, "Shall we play? Shall we play, Ismail?"

Of course, the border ran between us, that imaginary line created by the peaks of a low mountain range, which was no different from the others around, so that if you didn't know exactly where the "pyramids" were, you could, without noticing, cross to the other side. This was something that happened to many people, some of them even pretending they didn't know where the border was, especially hunters who would go over there in search of wild boar. For this reason too, the smuggling of tobacco and salt flourished before the war. People from Ayia Marina, Kastaniani, and Valtista, whose villages are right on the border, had relatives and friends on the Albanian site, and carried on with their lives. There were also those who went about at night, especially the people from Valtista. It appears that some old

---

[1] Translated into English by Derek Coltman, from the revised 1998 French edition (*Le Général de l'armée morte*), it was published in 2000 by the Harvill Press and republished in 2008 by Vintage. It concerns the search for and repatriation of the remains of Italian soldiers killed in Albania during the Second World War, the operation being led by a general. (Eds)

women, who were very poor, would also cross the border at night, in order to beg. In the same way, poor women would come over from the Albanian villages, even though they were more prosperous than ours. Perhaps because they were ashamed to beg in their own areas. The best known was "*Male*-Gousiaro",[2] a very tall, skinny old woman, shrivelled with age. She had two big glands, like eggs, hanging down from her neck. She would come laden with dried branches, and shout outside the courtyards. "Heather, heather for brooms. For your yards." In this way, she kept her dignity, and the women would give her a piece of bread for a handful of heather.

"Why do you want to lug *her* around with you?" they would ask about the girl who accompanied her — a big, sturdy, clumsy lass with a round face, and a rump as broad as a mare's. She was about twenty years old. "Male-Gousiaro" would always make a vague gesture, as if to say, "What can she do? She isn't all there."

"What's your name, eh?" they would ask the girl.

"Trygona, Trygona,"[3] she would quickly reply — they were the only words she knew. The children would follow them from door to door, making fun of them. In fact, they would be watching for when the women would slump down carelessly at a door to take a rest, because Trygona didn't wear anything underneath, and when she sat on the ground it was dark up inside. The mystery of her secret hair — isn't that so, Ismail?

The sight was strikingly revealing, for those who went at dawn to their fields, and, to take a short cut, went through the village field with the big walnut tree in the middle, under

---

[2] *Male* (two syllables) is an Albanian word for a grandmother or old woman.
[3] Meaning "turtledove". (Eds)

which the two women usually spent the night. Trygona would be asleep, having wrapped her head in her skirt, which she had pulled up, leaving her body exposed from the waist down, her rump naked to the frosty wind.

Then the sun would rise, as it did every morning at the same hour on the Mouzina and Aryirokastro mountains, and at midday, it would shine on the waters of the Drinos River, and on the cornfields of Deropolis.

We sowed corn too. We spent the nights of August in the fields, beside the fires lit for the wild boar, which would come out of Bouna forest, trample the corn, and destroy it. To pass the time, and to stop ourselves falling asleep, we would roast rocket plants on the embers, or sing the song that our grandmother taught us. Even *she* would be with us.

*On the plains of Deropolis,
The crabs get married.*[4]

And perhaps Ismail too, on the other side, sang the same song. Anyway, the two of us would certainly have called our grandmother *male*. Sometimes, the wild boar were tormented by hunger. They defied the fires, pounced on the corn, and began to munch it. Then we would leap on them, beating tins, and waving the lit torches high in the air. A dog would wake up and bark. Other dogs would reply from the neighbouring fields until, field by field, the barking, which went on all night, would reach the Albanian side.

"Yes," affirms Kadare, "the same thing happens in all Albanian villages. When one dog begins to bark, the others reply."[5]

[4] A satiric children's song, well known in Epirus, sung polyphonically to the accompaniment of the clarinet. (Eds)
[5] *The General of the Dead Army*, ch. XXI (Vintage edition p. 220). This and other quotations from Kadare's novel are not verbally identical to the text of the Vintage edition, having been translated into English from

The Occupation did away with the border. People came and went freely, and did legitimate business. Most of them went to barter for corn, because the Albanians had a large, well-watered plain, while our crops weren't enough to see us through the year. At that time, my family went over and sold a large double-blanket — we call it a "flokati"[6] today, that had been in our family for many years. I remember we got seventy *okas*[7] of corn for it. The number of people who went further inland to beg had increased. Going from village to village, they would arrive at Kastro, where the Turks would come out of their little houses and stone them, and set the dogs on them — including Ismail. But one doesn't remember these things with ill will — the actions of children, common in our own district too.

But I think it was from the Easter of 1939, that Ismail and I got to know each other better. Some time before — not very long, twenty-five years before — the village was divided between two landlords. Half of it was a large estate owned by a bey from Kastro, called Ahmet Dop, a fellow villager of Kadare's. The other half was the property of the monastery. At Easter, the villagers would gather together — united for once — and dance for three days in the large meadow belonging to the monastery. Anyway, on the afternoon of that Easter Monday in 1939, they were carousing under the big walnut trees. The tables were still laid out in a row, little piles of bones from the roast meat on the oil cloths, and among them glasses, with dregs of wine, greasy at the rim. The men had got fairly intoxicated, and the

Greek. Milionis either quotes a Greek translation or translates from the French — the book "came to us [...] from Paris" (page 47). (Eds)
[6] A kind of traditional white shaggy woven woollen blanket; they are now mostly used as rugs. (Eds)
[7] 1 oka = 1.28kg; 70 okas = 90kg. (Eds)

musicians, famous throughout the villages of Deropolis, were trying to make them dance again by playing dirges from Epirus. And as Kadare says,

> The clarinet began its lament once more. The violins accompanied it with their high-pitched tones, resembling women's voices.[8]

When he says this, he surely has in mind our songs, during which one man holds the tune, going on ahead, and then the women take it up. Nearby, a crowd of children were playing, shouting, and making a din the whole time.

Suddenly, the shouts and the instruments were silent. At the corner of the monastery, on the path that came from over the border, two Albanian officers appeared. They were tall and slim in their grey uniforms. If I were to meet them now, I would recognise their thin, bony, sunburnt faces. Everybody gathered round them, and brought them pieces of roast meat on a copper tray, and the jug of wine for a treat. They raised their heads high, showing their Adam's apples moving up and down. They were weeping. They wanted to say that they couldn't stomach the food. The Italians had invaded Albania.

From that day, until the end of '44 when liberation came, and the border went into place again — with barbed wire now, and fences with heavy patrols, so that you were as good as dead if you were caught anywhere near there — until '44 then, we lived through the same events as Ismail, who reminds me of them again in every detail — as if we were old friends, as I said in the beginning.

On the 28th of October 1940, the Italians invaded us as well.[9] By about midday, they had already reached the village.

---

[8] *The General of the Dead Army*, ch. XX (Vintage edition p. 204). (Eds)
[9] The Italians had occupied Albania much earlier, in April 1939.

They were rosy-cheeked and well-dressed, their uniforms neatly pressed, with a lot of iron stars on the lapels. They looked like bridegrooms. Among other things, that I won't mention now, the hens were in fear and dread. They cornered them in the narrow streets, caught them, and wrung their necks. Then they went round from house to house, with a bundle of hens on their backs, and asked to speak to the householder, in order to pay him in Albanian leks — nickel coins that had Victor Emmanuel in a helmet on one side, and on the other, the rods and the axe of Fascism — five leks for each chicken. We hadn't time to find out what value they really had. Besides, it was also a pretext for the Italians to go around the houses, and get into conversation with the householder, their eyes fixed on the windows, in case a romantic *ragazza*[10] would appear, with roses and doves, like the young girls on the shiny postcards that were sent to them from Rome and Naples, and that they would show to the villagers. Gradually, they all became bolder. In low voices, and with meaningful winks, they would ask, blushing, "C'è?" People would reply "Non c'è,"[11] and they would finish off in broken Greek, so as to be better understood and avoid trouble: "Here no! Yannena, Yannena." But as the war was still on in Kalamas, and Yannena was not yet occupied, the information seemed to them more like a challenge — something like "Go and get them!"[12] shall we say. Anyway, it seems that this kind of service that had been organised by General Staff "for

---

[10] Italian for "girl". (Eds)
[11] Italian for (in this context) "Are there any?" and "There aren't". (Eds)
[12] The Greek here is *molôn labe*, an Ancient Greek phrase said to have been uttered by Leonidas, one of the two kings of Sparta, during his heroic but doomed defence of the pass of Thermopylae, in 480 BC, with only about 7,000 men against Xerxes' invading Persian army 15–20 times that size.

reasons of strategy", as Kadare says,[13] hadn't time to reach our part of the country, and the girls remained in Aryirokastro.

> They installed them in a two-storey house, with a small garden around it, in the heart of the town . . . [14] Our town is very old. It has known many different kinds of epochs and customs. But never would we have expected such a thing. Something unheard of, something new and terrible, was hovering over our lives, as if the Occupation, with the barracks overflowing with a foreign army, and the hunger, didn't lie heavy enough on us. We didn't understand then, that this too was an aspect of war, like all the other aspects, and was neither worse nor better than the bombings, the hunger, and the barracks . . . [15] The Greek–Italian front was not far away, and at night we could hear the thunder of cannon . . . [16]

So, the girls stayed in Aryirokastro to await

> the soldiers returning from the front, filthy and unshaven. They stood in line, and didn't leave the queue, even when it began to rain. It was certainly easier to flush them out of the trenches, than out of that sad, meandering queue, that became unexpectedly longer . . . [17]

At least that is the perception that has prevailed. And later, Vincenzo, my fellow student in Thessaloniki, who is now a lecturer in Palermo, said to me, "The Italian loves music, flowers, and women. He doesn't want war." The women

---

[13] *The General of the Dead Army*, ch. VII, (Vintage edition p. 65). This and all the following quotations from Kadare's novel are from a long account of the setting up of an official Italian brothel in an Albanian village, as narrated by a café-owner. (Eds)
[14] *The General of the Dead Army*, ch. VII, (Vintage edition p. 68). (Eds)
[15] *The General of the Dead Army*, ch. VII, (Vintage edition p. 64). (Eds)
[16] *The General of the Dead Army*, ch. VII, (Vintage edition p. 70). (Eds)
[17] *The General of the Dead Army*, ch. VII, (Vintage edition p. 71). (Eds)

hadn't time to reach us, as I said before. But their regimental bands arrived. They were put into the village field, where, every afternoon, they played "Campagnola bella", the song that was later turned into "Mussolini the Fool" — that is to say, just a few days later, about the 20th of November. All night long, endless processions of Italian soldiers were returning now to the Albanian front, dragging themselves along behind the horses' tails. We were peeping out at them with a mixture of fear and joy, lifting the corner of the blanket that we had hung on the window. And when it had fully dawned, and the villagers began to venture outside the village for booty — eh, Ismail? — they found a dead man under every tree. Some half buried, others unburied, left there to rot without regimental bands, and without flowers, because that winter was harsh, with constant snow and ice. And when spring came — a black spring it was — it was all over.

It *wasn't* all over, of course. The Italians came back, different this time, without the good will and good humour they showed before. The first thing they said was, "No buono guerra."[18] They very quickly shut themselves up in their gendarmeries, and left the village empty for us, and the plain free for others. It was a short interval.

During this time, with the first hot days of summer, Trygona reappeared. She was alone now, without the old woman, and all swollen, with her belly up to her mouth. She appeared suddenly, without the children around her. She stood in the doorway, and leant against the door post. "Where have you sprung from, you whore? Who brought you to this plight?"

"Trygona, Trygona," she said, and stretched out her hand.

[18] Broken Italian: "War no good". (Eds)

"Who were you with? One of ours or an Italian?"

There was no point in asking her. Trygona gazed at us with a confused look in her eyes that were wilder now. She took the bread, and went away. We never saw her again. Who could be bothered to find out about Trygona? Besides, we too, on this side of the border, had learned

> that this was just another aspect of war, like all the others — neither better nor worse than the bombings and the hunger.[19]

As for the Italians, we almost forgot them, what with all the other things on our minds. Their bones were left scattered in the forests, and they rotted, or were bleached by the summer sun. For almost ten whole years, until, in 1951, an Italian mission came to collect and repatriate them. We helped them as much as we could. They went as far as Tepeleni, Kleisoura, and other places. Heading the mission was a general: *The general of the army of the dead*, in the words of my friend Kadare, who, in his book, reminded me of these and many other things. But what can we say. These are stories about the people of the Balkans. We like it the way it is now. "Let's go, boys. Let's go West."[20]

---

[19] *The General of the Dead Army*, ch. VII (Vintage edition p. 64), already quoted above, on p. 53. (Eds)

[20] The words in inverted commas are in English in the original. (Eds)

"Symphonia"

> *We who once crossed the roaring wave of the Aegean,*
> *are buried now in the boundless steppes of Ecbatana.*
> Philostratos[1]

Look what time brings about. A tourist trip, of the type that any lame Maria[2] can make these days — even more easily than I can, I would say — has brought me back at last to this ruined stairway without its balcony, and the old tiled roof which once covered it. What's even worse is that the house has gone. A stairway leading nowhere.

Last summer, some friends — well, hardly friends. Let's say acquaintances rather — pestered me to travel with them to the socialist countries — to see for ourselves what the system was like, and how people were getting on, so that we could draw our own conclusions, and not listen to somebody saying one thing, and somebody else another.

At first, I had my reservations. Such as: what would happen if we liked what we saw? were we going to start a revolution? or perhaps we would expel the multinationals, and the capitalists would let us change the system? and if, for example, we didn't like it, would we say that we were fine here, despite all our troubles?

But they were persistent. The real reason, of course, was for us to meet people, to see places with our own eyes. Everybody does this. Were we any different?

In the end, I declared myself a participant, and the group was complete.

---

[1] Sophist and rhetorician from Limnos (AD 170–250) who settled in Rome during the reign of Emperor Septimius Severus (193–211).
[2] Greek expression equivalent to "any Tom, Dick or Harry". (Eds)

It's pointless to talk about that endless coach journey, where everybody gazed out of the windows with one eye half-shut and the other closed, and about the empty feeling in the stomach, the ten-minute stops, when our bladders were bursting, the restaurants booked in advance that we had to eat at, with all the natural consequences. It's still more pointless to talk about the anecdotes and comments from certain people: silly retired officers — oh my God, what a breed — with their hanging dewlaps and white, short-sleeved shirts, with the brand name on the left pocket: "Okra, look everybody! We haven't seen okra anywhere."

We arrived at Budapest in the evening, and they installed us in a hotel, also called the "Budapest", near Moscow Square. It was a tall building, with about ten floors, and perfectly round, like a huge cylinder.

The next day, having been taken on a guided tour of the sights — the palaces and Saint Matthias Church,[3] which is reflected in the tinted glass of the Hilton Hotel, and then, after we had eaten at the Fisherman's Bastion,[4] on to Margaret Island,[5] the island of lovers — we ended up, in the evening, in the famous Váci Street, with its crystal, pottery, and camera shops. Here, the whole flock, hitherto passive, came suddenly to life and went wild, making a dash for the shop counters.

---

[3] "Saint Matthias" is what the original Greek text says (without "church"). In fact the church in question is dedicated to the Assumption of the Virgin Mary, but known, since its reconstruction in the nineteenth century, as "Matthias Church". However, the Matthias in question was not a saint but a fifteenth-century king of Hungary, a popular national hero, who married twice, both weddings being conducted in this church. (Eds)

[4] A restaurant with spectacular views over the city and the Danube. Its name in Hungarian is Halászbástya. (Eds)

[5] An island in the Danube in central Budapest. (Eds)

And so, left alone, I made my way to the Danube.

There, I found myself in front of Petőfi's statue.[6] I looked it over, and sat down on the pedestal. Then, I remembered that other poet, Attila József,[7] who also died young, in the midst of his poverty and his visions, and I thought that there must be, somewhere, a statue erected to him as well, and that I should ask, but I didn't know how to. Then I saw, coming towards me, a tall, sturdy, unshapely man with a limp. I thought this was my opportunity, but before I could open my mouth, he said, "Dollars? Dollars?" in a rough baritone voice. He wanted to buy dollars. I had already been informed about this trade by those officers on the coach. I had been irritated — for no other reason than that it was they who told me. "Leave me alone," I said to him in Greek. "Hey, you're a fellow countryman," he said, and grabbed my hand. He leant on the railing beside me, and we began to chat. There had been a shower of rain during the afternoon, and everything looked soft, shining like gold: the river flowing calmly, the suspension bridges, the big domes, and opposite, the green hill with the monument on its peak. "The Hill of Liberty," my fellow countryman told me. "Thirty thousand Soviets were killed there." I asked him about his limp. "The Albanian Campaign," he said. "The Albanian Campaign[8] and Grammos."[9] He was from a village in the Phlorina district. Then I asked him about the refugees, how many lived there, and what they thought about us. And suddenly, I was

---

[6] Sándor Petőfi (1823–1849) was a Hungarian poet noted for his passionate, rapturuous love of nature. He is Hungary's national poet and a revolutionary hero.

[7] József was one of the most important Hungarian lyric poets of the 20th century. His socialist themes were inspired by his love of mankind.

[8] The war between Greece and Italy (1940–1941) was fought mainly on Albanian soil.

[9] The fiercest battles of the Greek Civil War took place on Mt Grammos.

overtaken by a quietly erosive desire, a yearning, I would say, to go and see them where he said they lived, in Tatabánya, Miskolc, and the village of Beloiannisz. We agreed on the village. He promised he would send me a taxi in the morning, and would arrange a good price for me.

So the next morning, when the group was gathering for the coaches in front of the hotel — Lake Balaton was on the programme — my taxi driver arrived. He had my name written on a little card, and was looking for me. I didn't tell them anything about my destination — better to be cautious, I thought. It was necessary, however, to justify my not going with them. We really did get on well together with our jokes, which is hardly surprising. We Greeks carry Greece with us wherever we go — but they would have to excuse me. I had to have a check-up — no, no, nothing serious, but here was an opportunity for me to see where I stood, as regards my health. And suddenly, they all wanted to do that too. It was an opportunity for them to come in the same taxi, and it would cost me less. I locked the door from the inside, and we drove off, while they were still talking to the driver through the closed window.

After an hour's drive — the wet grass smelt pleasant with a peppery aroma that I remember to this day — we arrived at the village with the single-storey houses and the high roofs, that the Greek refugees[10] had built thirty years ago. I got out in the square, and my taxi driver showed me on his watch that I had to be there in one hour, at the same spot. Then I went and stood alone in the middle of the square. Silent figures began to come out of the doors around. They were grey-haired, hollow-cheeked, old. I don't want to talk about things that one is not permitted to discuss — the

---

[10] In 1949, after the leftist forces were defeated in the Civil War, large numbers of Greeks fled to the communist countries of Eastern Europe.

suspicious looks and the underlying panic. I'll mention only the cemetery beyond the little wood, with the acacia and cypress trees, and the photographs on the upright marble slabs — old men with drooping moustaches, old women with black kerchiefs tied tightly under their chins: Dimitrios Raptis, Evanthia Rapti, and around it, the endless plain.

Two refugees escorted me to the café to have a brandy, while Greek children played in the streets, chattering in Hungarian. The men stopped playing backgammon and cards, and gathered at our table. Only one decrepit old man, all skin and bone, showed no sign of leaving his chair in front of the window. He sat there motionless all the time, his hands leaning on a crudely-made stick, and gazed into the distance, towards the Danube, which wasn't visible — only the plain. You could see that it was tiring for him to control his jaw, because every so often he would make an attempt to close it, and then he would wipe it with a dirty little kitchen cloth, one of those cloths with a checked pattern that he had thrown over his knee. I asked who he was.

"Ah," they said, "Uncle Mitsos Doulias." I couldn't believe my eyes. I approached him, and put my hand on his shoulder.

"How are you, uncle?" I asked him.

He moved his head, and managed to say, "I don't know you."

I told him my name. "You've grown," he said.

All the time we were drinking raki, I was thinking of Doulias' balcony, the stair head where I used to sit with him, and gaze out. And I remember that, as I gazed, I would be recalling the things he had told me — that behind that distant mountain was the sea, all blue — "an upside-down sky", he would say, to make me understand. It seemed to me that he was talking about worlds that were very far away, actually behind the setting sun, which at that hour sat on the mountain peak. Doulias, lying on his divan, in summer, half-reclining, his elbow on the pillow, his head resting on his palm, would be gazing out too.

"Uncle, why does the sun turn red when it goes down behind the mountain?"

"Because that's Albania over there, where the reds are." And he would add, "Not like us here."

Then I would try to recall some of our villagers who, I knew, had come from Albania in the old days. It struck me that their faces actually did have something reddish about them, but then again there wasn't a great difference. What difference could there be? All our faces were baked by the sun, and by harsh living — veritable frying pans, they were. I would tell Doulias about my speculations. "Never mind them," he would reply. "They've been here so many years, they're mongrels. They've gone dark, like us."

"What colour flag has Albania, uncle?"

"Hm, what colour? Red. What else would it be?"

"Aah, of course."

As a consequence, I could see a big red flag, made of silk, stretching throughout the whole western sky, and on it was the sun, which was even redder. I told him this, and it pleased him.

"One thing, though," he said. "Don't tell the others. They don't understand."

Where would I tell it? Who else had the desire to sit and gaze at the sun and the sky? It wasn't a year yet since the Germans had left, and everybody was struggling to put their burnt houses in order, to get a roof over their heads. Only myself and Doulias had the desire to sit and gaze. His house, being at the end of the village, escaped the fire. "Even the Germans didn't think much of it," he would say.

Before the war, he had worked in a bakery in Athens. They said he was the first Syndicalist. The police had their eye on him. Metaxas[11] sent him to the island of Ikaria, they said, and he educated himself there. He had an elderly mother in the village, so bent over, that her nose nearly touched the ground. Every Saturday, when the postman came, there she was at the café, leaning on a crooked piece of wood that she used as a stick. "Tell me, will my Mitsos, God save him, bring equality? Will he straighten the country out?" The villagers would joke cruelly that he would straighten out the body of the old woman as well. But when Doulias came to the village, as did so many Athenians during the Occupation, he found his house closed up. He was too late for her.

They would tell these stories about him, and say that he was a mysterious man. That wooden balcony with the tiled roof had become, for the villagers, something like a calendar, which showed the two main seasons, winter and summer, the only ones that were of any interest in our village, because they stood out. As soon as autumn came, and Mourgana clouded over, Doulias would nail up the door of his house where the balcony was, and go to the ground floor room to hibernate. During this time, he would go in and out of the entrance under the stairway, although, to be precise, he was rarely seen going in and out in the winter. "Doulias is dead to the world," they would say. "He's as docile as the Russian bear."

However, there were others who said he did this for fear you would see that he didn't go out of his house during the day. It was a tactic, so as not to draw attention to himself. But at night, when the wind blew and it rained, when you

---

[11] Yoannis Metaxas was appointed Greek prime minister in 1936 and soon dismissed Parliament and ruled as a dictator until his death in 1941.

couldn't see your nose in the dark, and not a soul dared to poke their head out of the door, he met with other cadres of the Laka region, in Megalo Rema, at Aliousis' mill, where they had discussions. All those years, he had been an ELAS partisan. They said, among other things, that he was the one who gave the commands.

Anyway, as soon as spring came, he would move his paraphernalia up to his lookout: an old divan with a thin metal frame, his bedding made of fibre and straw, and a towel, black with dirt, lying beside the flattened pillow. And close to hand on the floor, with its roughly-hewn planks, was the jar of cold water. He would commandeer any child he saw passing in the street. "Hey, young fellow-me-lad! Take the jar, and fill it at the tap." Indeed, most times he would send *me*. I did it with pleasure, because then he would let me sit on the balcony, and tell me about Jimmy Londos,[12] who had won the diamond belt. Ironically, they called me Jimmy Londos too, because I was the skinniest child in our village. We had been through the Occupation, and were all more or less in bad health, but mine was very bad. Anyway, he had a photo of Jimmy Londos in a big faded magazine, and he would show me him holding his arms out to the side, with the muscles bulging, as if he were lifting two huge buckets, although he wasn't lifting anything. That magazine even had pictures of the first flyers — Icarus falling into the sea, in a flurry of scattered wings, and underneath, Daedalus, with his face in his hands. "I've been on the Ikarian Sea," Doulias would tell me. "These aren't fairy tales. *They* were the first flyers. That's the way it goes. They're killed, then others come along and claim to be the pioneers."

So I took pleasure in bringing him cold water, and

---

[12] A Greek wrestling champion before the Second World War who took part in wrestling matches in the USA as well as Greece.

watching him drink it eagerly. He drank water all the time, and sweated all the time, but always on one side of his face. He would keep on wiping the sweat with the towel.

Then, I heard that his lungs were infected, or rather, one of his lungs, on the side where he sweated. "Are you out of your mind, child? Don't go near him. He's consumptive, and you'll catch it from him," said that Kaphiris with the quiff and the dark glasses. He was so small and fat that they called him "the Punch", like the tool. "And he's a Marxist," he added.

Yet one couldn't say for sure that he was ill. He would work in the gardens the whole morning, from spring to autumn. "My work is seasonal," he would say. He would tidy up little stone hedges at Megalo Rema with his pickaxe, build them up into dry stone walls, to strengthen them, open a trench for water to flow, and then he would sell the plots, or rent them for growing vegetables. He began work at dawn, when it was still dark, and returned to the village towards noon, with an old cap worn askew, and the towel thrown over his shoulder. "Eight hours," he'd say. "*I* won't break the eight-hour day. Blood has flowed for it." And he would tell me about May Day in Chicago, and about the three "eight hours" — eight hours work, eight hours recreation, and eight hours sleep. "This is my relaxation," he would say, "reading and sitting here looking out." Later, I used to think that if I hadn't, after all, caught tuberculosis — although for a period I had a suspicion that I might have — I must at least have caught these habits from him. He would read old, faded booklets that he hid under his mattress: "The Permanent Revolution", "The Worldwide Proletariat", "When the People Awake" — always that kind of thing. "If the people aren't educated, you can't expect progress. What progress could you make with a Punch? He can't see anything except lace knickers. But the capitalists don't let us open our eyes, so that we are in their hands."

"What is capitalism, uncle?"

"A monster. Like the Hydra of Lerna,[13] do you understand?" And then he would explain what he meant: "Do you know the cataract at Megalo Rema? A treasure. White coal. Do you know what white coal means? Electric light for all the villages in Laka, so that the whole region would be shining. And the oil in Lavdani — why do you think they don't dig it out? To have us under their thumb, by selling us oil from the Middle East. The Italians said it too. 'You have enough oil here,' they said, 'to drown Europe.' And why, do you think, the Italians made war? For the oil in Albania and Lavdani. In Albania, they acted in time, and took the oil out, and now they've got electric light. Do you see the villages of Deropolis in the evening? All lighted by electricity."

I can't confirm that those villages had electric light as early as that. As I said, it was the period immediately after the Occupation, and it's rather doubtful. Well, I doubt it today, but I had no doubt then — nor, do I imagine, had he. Their lights twinkled enchantingly all over the plain of Deropolis, like constellations that the sky had emptied onto it.

Anyway, with all these things he told me, and with everything I heard about him, I finally came to the conclusion that Doulias was not like other people. For this reason, when I heard one day that he had disappeared — during that time, rumours were circulating about certain

---

[13] In mythology, a monster water serpent with the body of a hound and anything from five to five hundred heads. Slain by Hercules as his "Second Labour". (Driven mad by the goddess Hera, Hercules killed his five children and was commanded by his father-in-law, Creon, King of Thebes, to perform the Twelve Labours.)

groups of people who had appeared near Kasidiaris, and had headed for Mourgana — it seemed perfectly natural to me, like something that one had to expect. "He's gone," they said. "He's gone over with the others." And some said, "Doulias has given us the slip." Kaphiris even shouted it out in the middle of the village.

From that time on, everything was chaos. If you asked me who was alive, and who had died, I wouldn't have known what to tell you — people scattered, and the country was ruined — until I went on that journey, and there was Doulias, a ghost from the past, beside the window.

But now it seemed the hour had passed, and the driver came into the café looking sulky, and asking for me. As I held his cold hand to say goodbye, the old man managed to ask, "My house? Is it still there?"

What could I say to him? I assured him that at the first opportunity, I would go to our village. As soon as I went back there, I would sit on his balcony and wait for him. He nodded his head. He agreed.[14]

And now here I am, in his "house", on this ruined stone stairway without the balcony, and without the house — a stairway leading nowhere, as I said. I am sitting on the stairhead, just gazing out and smoking a Hungarian cigarette from the packet they gave me at the café when they were seeing me off. Its smell reminds me of the peppery aroma of the wet grass. It's a white packet, with a red and black pattern, and a lyre on the top. ARA 9.60 — that's the price, 9.60 florins, say about twenty drachmas. The brand is SYMPHONIA.[15] And beside me, Doulias. I have brought

---

[14] In the Greek "He agreed" is *Symphonise* (four syllables). Compare the story's title, whose significance is revealed in the next paragraph. (Eds)

[15] This brand name, like the title of the story, is in Latin characters in the original Greek. (Eds)

him back to his balcony, and have made him lie down on the divan — the only thing that it was in my power to do.

Phryni

Our Phryni did not have the pallor of the ancient flute player.[1] A pallor which, in man's strange imagination, was the reason for giving the name of the toad, the most repulsive animal, to the most divine creature, "the most beautiful courtesan of all time", who had inspired an Apelles[2] to paint the Anadyomene Aphrodite, and a Praxiteles[3] to make the Cnidus statue of her. At least, that's what the Encyclopaedia said — three volumes in all, the only ones remaining in our house. Then, these too were lost during the terrible events that followed. But I still remember the page with the naked statue, that had been dampened by the perspiration from my hands, so that it too had taken on Aphrodite's pallor.

Our Phryni had a dark complexion, browned in the sun, and eyes that cast dark, lustrous glances. And as for her body . . . Now that I think about it all, here in my apartment in Ippokratous Street, I must have been the luckiest person in that world of the "closed rural community", as those who have studied the subject call it, when they talk about that time, which, they say, is lost for ever. With comments like that, they make me feel that I am the last witness or, to put it another way, the person who has been given this privilege.

---

[1] Phryne (4th century BC) was a famous courtesan from Thespiae in Boeotia.
[2] Apelles (4th century BC) was regarded as the greatest of all the Ancient Greek painters. None of his work survives. The Aphrodite Anadyomene (Aphrodite Rising [from the waves]) was one of his most famous pictures.
[3] Praxiteles (also 4th century BC) was a leading Athenian sculptor. His most famous statue was the Aphrodite of Cnidus, known from the many Roman copies.

Anyhow, our life was indeed so rural that it was full of the smell of horse manure and rutting animals, and was so confined that, if you dared to cross the village boundaries, you would most probably have found yourself in front of the hollow eyes of German machine guns that crouched in their lairs, guarding the roadways. Those who had got out of Athens on time, and had come to the village, ate bread and were content — even though there was no way out, on pain of death. Others had been blockaded "in Athens and dying of hunger" — an expression that showed very vividly that the consequences were fatal, an inevitable necessity, like its rhyme *Athina* and *peina*.[4] At that time, most men from our parts would be away from their villages. Now and then, they would come back, make a woman pregnant, and go off again. There was no work for them in the area.

One of these was Phryni's father. Their house was beside ours, almost next door, but I can't remember him at all, perhaps because I had never seen him. I even doubt if Phryni herself had ever known him. There was only his photograph, always in its place, above their fireplace, hanging on a thorny twig. He was a tall, dark man, with almond-shaped eyes. Phryni certainly resembled him.

"When the war's over, he'll take us to Athens too," she would say. When she said "us", she meant her mother — a silly, babbling, skinny woman, who used to create a racket with her shouting and fussing from five in the morning until she went off to work in the fields. Sometimes, she would take Phryni with her, but most times, she worked in company with other women, and left Phryni in the house to do the other work. What other work? Only a bit of sweeping, since there was usually no question of making a meal.

I was then, I think, fourteen years old. I had started

---

[4] *Athina* is the Modern Greek form of "Athens"; *peina* means "hunger".

Secondary School — a five-hour journey on foot — and since the roads were closed, I had only the title of Secondary School pupil for the time being. My only book, the depleted Encyclopaedia I was talking about, was inherited from my uncle who was educated, and had died before the war, in Athens, of tuberculosis, I think. I don't know a lot about him. They didn't talk much in our house.

Outside the village, there was a deep ravine beneath a huge precipice, where birds of prey nested, and all around there was dense vegetation: large maple trees, plane trees, and elm trees, covered with wild vine and clematis, so that Phryni and I would get lost in the damp, sunless footpaths. Then the gardens began — little stone hedges among cherry and walnut trees, going down to the stream below, with its maidenhair and large willows leaning over the water that flowed nimbly away, after it had first been churned up into a white cloud by the huge waterfall. We all used to water our gardens together, and then go down to the stream.

Usually only the boys went down there — Kolas, Machos, Gondos, and myself — without Phryni, Vito, and Marianthi. When it got hot, and our goats were resting, we would take off our clothes and go into the cloud, the waterfall driving frozen needles into our thin bodies, and the stream echoing with our shouts.

I used to weave baskets there with Phryni. Only the two of us. We put the willow wands in a basin of water, in little bundles, pressed down with stones, to soak them, and we would sit beneath the big elm tree with the ivy. Phryni would show me how to make patterns — first, five rows of green wands, and then three more, peeled white. At midday, the sun would climb high. The heat was stifling, even down there. She would then gather her frock above her knees and paddle in the cold water, until her feet turned pink. War?

Hunger? Bombings? Fear? Massacres? None of that came down there.

One day, in the middle of summer, when the place was seething with cicadas, Phryni suddenly groaned, and threw away her basket. "Aah, I'm suffocating," she said, and tossed back her head. And then she said, "I'm going into the waterfall." Her eyes shone. I was speechless, standing with my mouth open. She went behind some heather bushes, and threw her frock on the branches. She was left only with a white petticoat. And then, stooping over, she climbed the rocks that were slippery with moist vegetation. The white cloud of water enveloped her, and she began to shriek, her cries drowning in the roar of the waterfall. Only when I called out, "Phryni, you'll slip," did I hear her say, "You come too." But I pretended I hadn't heard her.

When she got down, and came nearer, her wet petticoat had become transparent, and was clinging to her body. She wasn't wearing anything else. She was laughing and trembling. She went behind the heather bushes, and called to me, "Turn your head away now, and don't look, or heaven help you!" I did turn away, but turned round again at one moment and saw her, as I had never seen her, even in my dreams. She slowly put on her dry frock. Then she came and stood beside me, laughing. "Look at you," she said. "*I* went into the water, and you're the one who's trembling."

From that day, I avoided being with her, making the excuse that I had some reading to do, when she would call me to come and water the gardens. I would be immersed in the Encyclopaedia, studying that fleeting vision of her in her statues — the Anadyomene and the Cnidus Aphrodite. I haven't been back to the stream — for forty years now.

In any case, in a few days everything changed. There was a big sabotage operation on the main road, and the partisan auxiliaries — our villagers in fact — drove some German supply trucks outside the village, and set fire to them there. Beset with fear, we made for the thick forests and riverbeds. But the Germans were slow to attack. About twenty days passed, and they didn't fire one shot. They were preparing something else for us this time.

During this interval, we were living a very different life in the woods. Most of the animals had scattered, and had become common property. Whoever found them, milked them. And of course, our houses had become common property as well, with whatever remained in them, and the unharvested vineyards — it was August — and the vegetable gardens. Everything was at the disposal of those who dared go secretly into the village, where there was the danger of finding themselves face to face with the Germans. They would bring sacks filled with whatever they had had time to grab, and those who happened to be nearby when they returned, gathered round them, and the things were shared out. We all had flour, some more than others, and we baked at night in the caves, so that the smoke and the fire wouldn't be seen.

After the first few days, we began to organize our lives somewhat. Relatives and neighbours gathered in separate hiding places with their belongings. With our neighbours, we gathered together the few sheep and goats that we had. We made up a little flock, and at night we shut them up in an old sheep pen that had been buried in the thicket for who knows how long. We slept there beside it, and guarded it. At dawn, we took the animals out to graze, until it became hot. We then brought them down to drink at the riverbed, which still had a little water in mid-summer. So we were together again: Kolas, Machos, myself, Gondos. And Phryni, Vito, and Marianthi as well.

When it came to midday, the animals rested in the shade, under the big plane trees, and we would throw ropes of goat hair over the branches, to make swings for the girls. We would quarrel over who would push them the most, and we would quarrel especially over Phryni. I obviously thought that I had most right, since our houses were very close together, practically next door — but what houses now? Phryni would find excuses to give my turn to Gondos, even though she would call him "Liabi" when they argued. This was because his grandfather had come from Libochovo[5] in Albania, a long time ago, and as we know, children don't forget so quickly. Gondos always wore a smock without sleeves, day and night, the same one, black with dirt. He would put his bare arms firmly around Phryni, pull her back against him, and then push her way up high, higher than any of us could. Overcome with the thrill of it, she would laugh, throwing her head back, and touching the leafy boughs with her feet.

It was the month of August, and boiling hot. The billy-goats were roused, and were chasing the females. The air stank of goats. Gondos had a huge billy-goat, as big as a heifer. Often, he used to ride on him. The animal would trot along as haughty as a despot, with Gondos on his back, his feet hanging down. The billy-goat's beard hung down too, yellow with urine, because when the rutting instinct seized him, he would stretch his penis way out and lick it, until his beard was soaked. Then he would raise his head up towards the sky, and sniff the air in ecstasy, his upper lip raised. The arch of filth watered Gondos himself, hitting him from a distance.

This same billy-goat got us into trouble, because he would disturb the females, and they would scatter away from

---

[5] Libohovë in Albanian. (Eds)

their resting place. That afternoon, he gave chase to one of them. She wouldn't stay still for him, nor would he leave her alone. From her bell, we knew that she was Phryni's. Phryni got angry. "Run, or I'll lose her. The wolves'll eat her." Gondos was laughing heartily. She became more determined. "Run, will you! Liabi, filthy swine," she shouted. Suddenly, Gondos looked grim. He jumped up, took a short cut through the footpaths, stepped out in front of the two animals, and made them come to us. Then he grabbed her bell, and held her by the horns, her head between his legs. The billy-goat, all excited, leapt forward and mounted her, right there in front of us, his tongue hanging out, almost licking Gondos' face. When he got down, the goat was huddled into a trembling ball. During all this, Phryni didn't stop shouting despairingly, "Leave her alone! Leave her alone!" And when it was over, she said, "You filthy swine," and burst into tears. The other girls sulked as well. We became silent. Phryni wouldn't raise her eyes to look at us. I felt very wounded. We didn't exchange a word until the evening, when we gathered the animals together and shut them into the pen. Then Kolas' father came running down the mountainside, shouting that the Germans were burning our villages. The whole area was glowing, over in the forests, behind the ridges.

It's all been forgotten now. Only *I* still remember, as I go up and down the steps to my apartment in Ippokratous Street, where not a single child's voice is heard, as though life had stopped. And Phryni, an Aphrodite turned to marble, like those fashioned by Apelles and Praxiteles.

The last tanner

To the memory of Dimitris Chadzis[1]

Mermingas the shoemaker went round every inn in Kritharopazaro. He took a quick look through the glass panelling of the Glass Café — what would Charisis be doing here? What would he be poking his nose in here for? He came to the Crow Inn, and asked there too.

"Has Charisis the tanner been here by any chance?"

"We haven't seen him," they said.

He went back to Kritharopazaro. He looked once more in Zoïs' inn, and asked again if Charisis had called in the meantime. "He hasn't appeared," they told him, and he went down towards the lake. It was really dark now. The electric lights had been on for some time. And it was bloody damp. The south wind was blowing, chilling you through to the bone. The sky and lake were both pitch-black. He would hear the lake roaring, and spewing up the waves at the pier — the bastard had stirred up some filth, and wouldn't rest easy until it had dumped it on the reeds. Going up to Kourmanio, he looked in at the cafés one by one, and arrived at Gouyannos' cook shop, from where he had set out.

"I've been all round," he told them. "No luck."

They looked at him open-mouthed: Zoïs the innkeeper,

---

[1] This story, first published in the journal *Andi* vol. 83 (1981), was written as a tribute to the writer Dimitris Chadzis, almost immediately after his death on the 20th of July 1981. It contains references to some of the stories in Chadzis' *The end of our small town* (English translation by David Vere, Birmingham 1995). In one of these stories 'Sioulas the Tanner", Chadzis writes about the fraternity of tanners in Yannena. At the end of "The last tanner" there is an implied reference to Chadzis himself.

Karabinas the hairdresser, commonly known as "wagtail", Katsoulis the coachman, Griboyannis the tinsmith, Siëmos the gunsmith. The pieces of liver on the large plate were nearly cold. And the glasses were full.

"Why are you looking at me like idiots? I couldn't find him anywhere." Behind the counter, Gouyannos too was standing, pot-bellied and greasy, his wooden spoon suspended in the air.

"It doesn't look good to me," he said. But the others rebuked him.

"Get away with you," they said to him. "The man's been held up somewhere. We'll begin. He'll show up any minute now. What else would he do?" They stuck the forks into the liver, and dipped the bread in the oil with their fingers. "Here's to us," they said. "Cheers." But the wine wouldn't go down.

"What the devil's the matter with you?" said Zoïs. "You can't even drink half a carafe."

"If we had Charisis here now, it would be different."

There was a long silence. A silence that became unbearable, as hopes that he would appear faded.

"The old tanner has played truant on us," Katsoulis burst out at last. "If he were here this evening, it would be different. He knew stories with meaning to them, and he had a way of telling them. He knew all about the people in old Yannena, the 'liver-eaters' who wouldn't set out for work in the morning, until they had called at the cook shop first — liver and a half-carafe, all at the same time."

"Great times — just like we have."

"What do you mean, 'just like we have'? Once every Saturday evening, and you say 'just like we have'. They were different people."

"He even knew about the lady Vasilo, that the klephts

carried off to make Vlachleidis[2] send ransom money, and afterwards they made up a song about her:

> *It is no crime, it is no wrong, nor is it yet a sin —*
> *Vasio may live there in the hills, and in the lairs of klephts.*

"Come on Siëmos, sing it from the beginning."

"I can't now," said Siëmos. They were silent.

He was one of the old ones. He had lived through these things, and could talk about them. He knew the old families, the Molyvades and Sabethaï Kabilis,[3] who was responsible for what happened to the Jews, that time with the Germans. "Come on," they said to him. "Let's get our people quietly out of the town, and go to Zagori."[4] But Kabilis *would* go his own way, and do what *he* thought should be done, using the law as far as he could, and bribing this one and that one. He wouldn't take them up to the mountains, where the partisan war was raging.

"*I* remember Kabilis," said Katsoulis. "And Margarita Molyvada,[5] I remember *her*. I used to drive her in the phaeton. Then the Germans executed her. But Charisis would tell it differently. He had his own way of telling things."

---

[2] Klephts were Greek brigands who were active during the Ottoman period and many klephts played a part in the Greek War of Independence (1821–1829). Their exploits inspired many folk ballads. Vlachleidis was the head of a well-to-do family in Yannena. The abduction of Vasilo (or Vasio) Vlachleidi took place in the 19th century.

[3] The leader of the Jewish community in Yannena. The Jews referred to in the story were rounded up and sent to Auschwitz where they perished. Sabethaï Kabilis is also the eponymous hero of a story by Chadzis.

[4] From a Slav root meaning "beyond the mountains", Zagori is the name of a region with forty-six villages between Yannena and the Albanian border. (Eds)

[5] One of the last members of an old family. She was also the heroine of a story by Chadzis under the name "Margarita Perdikari".

"And as for politics, very knowledgeable. An idealist."

"Like us."

"What do you mean, 'like us'? Which of us went up into the mountain, like Charisis? Us? We were only roughed up a bit at the police station. Are you saying he's like us?"

"A fine man in every way. Whenever he saw a woman, he would twirl his moustache. He would tell that one about the Jewish girls. "Heh, wagtail, how did he tell it?'"

"Oh! the one about Rebecca! Last night, when my husband was out, a gentleman comes to the house, and opens the door. And what did you do? I let him in, to see what he'll do. He takes off his coat, and hangs it, like a gentleman, on the peg. I let him, to see what he'll do. He takes me to the bed. He takes off his clothes, and he takes off mine. I let him, to see what he'll do. He lies on top of me, and puts something between my legs. What are you doing there? I say to him . . ." The hairdresser's words hung in the air. Nobody laughed. They went silent, their eyelids drooping, heavy with wine. Poor Charisis, how he could tell the stories. His face would light up with laughter. He loved the good things in life, the old bachelor. He never tired of the women.

On Saint John's Day,[6] he would go around the neighbourhoods in the evening, from fire to fire. The women would drag him here, there and everywhere to make him sing for them "Grand, you see, grand carnivals". And that other one he sang, acting it out too:

How do they grind the pepper, those diabolic monks?[7]

---

[6] The Day of John the Baptist, 24 June, just after the summer solstice, when fires are lit in the villages. It is said that girls who jump over the fires will see the man they are to marry.

[7] This is a song with actions, the most comical of which involves moving along the ground on your buttocks.

"Come on, Charisis, show us how they grind the pepper. Here's to you!"

"Here's to you, Charisis," they said, and brought the glasses to their lips.

But he used to tell an even better one about the tanners. How they would tan the hides in the lake, behind the timber-yards, up to their knees in filthy, foul-smelling water, and their trousers unbuttoned, to give their testicles an airing. And they'd be telling dirty jokes all the time. They had their odd habits, their eccentricities. But at home, they behaved like proper householders. And were respected in the marketplace. That Sioulas — a perfect gentleman. They're all gone. The merchants have taken their place. The leather's no good now. The world's not honest anymore. There's only Charisis now, the last tanner... The conversation stopped short again. They were silent. They looked at each other with clouded eyes. They all felt sad.

"Come, cheers! Damn you, Gouyannos, you bastard. You're giving us short measure." And Griboyannis held out the earthenware jug towards the cook's counter.

Gouyannos said, "Are you not going to see how the man is?" Suddenly, as if alarmed, they got up and went to the door one by one. They walked down towards the lake, to the old tanneries, one behind the other, with heads bent, heavy with wine. Old men in their wide, patched trousers — except for Karabinas the barber who was walking in front, swaying with a mincing gait. Neither the south wind nor the damp bothered him. He knew all the alleys and all the secret doors, did the wagtail. "His house is beyond the timber-yards, behind the old Synagogue. I know where it is." And he kept turning round and motioning them to follow him, the old carbine,[8] the old breech-loader. Not being able to keep up with him in the deserted streets exasperated them.

They cut through the timber-yards that smelt of wet sawdust, and squeezed into a narrow, forgotten alleyway. Karabinas stopped at a small, half-open door. The others gathered round him. Nobody dared to go in. They just gazed at the old house with the thin, collapsing wall, and ruined window above the door — was there a light inside, or was it coming from the electric lamp at the corner, with its tin hat that the wind shook, producing a mournful creaking? Nobody could make up their mind to push the door open. Karabinas, once he had shown them the house, stood back and didn't stir.

Siëmos was the first to make a move, the others following close behind. The entrance was pitch-dark. It smelt musty. But in the corner, there was a stairway that was dimly lit, every now and then, by a light that was coming down from above. Stumbling, they began to climb, and at every step they took, the wooden stairway lamented, like the lament that rose with them towards the small room. They saw a divan in the middle, with two large candles, and between them Charisis, lying peacefully, half-smiling beneath his white moustache. The men huddled into a corner. Two old women were sitting on stools, their hands folded in their aprons. They only raised their eyes. After a moment, one of them said, "Poor Charisis. Your friends have come."

As if they had just understood, they slowly raised their hands, made the sign of the cross, and then stood motionless and embarrassed.

"Why are you standing like that?" said the old woman again. "Why don't you sit down?"

---

[8] The name Karabinas comes from the Italian *carabina* meaning "rifle", like the English "carbine". (Eds)

They all looked round them. Then they settled down, two on the floor, two at the fireplace, which was covered up by a curtain, an old piece of dark cloth — it would have been years since a fire was lit. Siëmos and Griboyannis remained standing, legs apart, arms hanging down.

"It's well you've come," said the second woman. She nodded to the other, who got up too.

"It's as well you've come, so that we can go home, and get some sleep. We're neighbours . . . we're about to faint with the smell of that damned wine that's coming from you. Take the stools."

"We'll be here early tomorrow."

And while one went down the stairs, the second one followed limply, one hip rising, the other falling, pitching and tossing like a boat tied up at the pier. She was grumbling, "What tomorrow? There aren't even three hours of night left."

The women went away, and, sitting cross-legged, with Charisis in the middle, the men relaxed.

"You shouldn't have done this to us, brother," said Siëmos. Charisis smiled wanly, as if sadly, in the feeble light shed by the candles.

"We should have lit the lamp . . ."

Mermingas took down the little glass lamp that was hanging from a nail on the wall, beside the fireplace. He shook it. There was some oil in it. He lit it. A soft light spread over the blackened walls, over the cupboard with the glass panel, over the gaunt faces with their swollen, bovine eyes. And the time began to roll along quietly and cosily, each man thinking his own thoughts — if he had anything to think about. The cold came in through all the cracks, forcing the men to huddle together, and pull their heavy, much-mended jackets around them, each squeezed into his own little space.

At one moment, Karabinas, who was sitting at the hearth, stretched out his hand and lifted the curtain — a spontaneous movement, to see if they could light something to warm them. His hand caught a demijohn. He shook it. They heard a splashing sound.

"Poor Charisis," he said. "He keeps the raki here." His roguish eye hovered around the glass cupboard. He glided over to it with a cat-like movement, and opened it. Among empty bottles, he found three liqueur glasses.

"We'll have one," he said. "For the sake of custom."

First, he filled the three glasses. Those sitting next to him, took them — "May God rest his soul," they said. Then he did the same for the other three. The raki went down, warming them up nicely. "Raki — and it's the strong stuff. He always liked the good things in life." Their faces became flushed.

"Get up, Karabinas," said Mermingas suddenly. "Put out those candles. I can't stand them. The bloody things are choking us with their smoke." Karabinas glided over like a cat again, and put out the candles. Before he sat down, he gathered up the glasses, then went back to where he was sitting at the fireplace, and filled them again — for the second round. Then, Siëmos softly began to murmur a sad song, like a dirge.[9]

> *Rise up, my Yannos, do not sleep so deeply*
> *The heavens are pouring down, and you'll get wet...*

"Siëmos!" Griboyannis interrupted him. "Not doleful songs for Charisis — 'In Yannena in Kourambas'. We'll sing that."

---

[9] *Miroloyi* in Greek: a lament sung or recited at funerals. Professional mourners have a repertoire of *miroloyia* from which to draw inspiration for their own spontaneous verses.

And they all began together, as they did at Gouyannos' on their Saturday evenings —

In Yannena in Kourambas, there is a little swallow . . .

— their voices hoarse, uncoordinated, cracked by pain.

Zoïs interrupted the song again: "Karabinas, you wagtail, give us the demijohn. I can't look at you fussing with it the whole time, over there at the fireplace, like a tinsmith at his saucepan. Put it here in the middle, and we'll fill the glasses and drink like men, so that Charisis can see us, and his soul can rejoice." His words flowed into a song — "One Sunday . . ." — and the others followed him:

One Sunday, on a holy day
there came a dove —
would that I had not seen her . . .

Then they sang "Phezos, you tyrant, you didn't like Yannena". They continued with "Vasiliki is in command, vizier Alipasha".[10] And then "Siamandakas",[11] until their voices grew hoarse and they couldn't sing anymore. One by one, they were silent, but not immediately. First, they would sing only up to the middle of the song, then a line here and there, then single words, and after, odd syllables, in the end they slumped to the floor and were asleep, another world went out with them, until a deep peace spread over the room. The oil in the lamp was finished. The flame rose up once or twice to the top of the lamp chimney, to get a breath

---

[10] Lady Vasiliki (1793–1835) was the daughter of the klepht Kitsos Kondaxis. She was abducted by Ali Pasha in 1805, and became his wife. She used his goodwill towards her for the benefit of Christians.

[11] Like the other songs mentioned in this story, this is an old folk song from Epirus. It is also a dance for men. The song celebrates the bravery of a fine and handsome young Albanian man, Osman Taka (Siamandakas in Greek), who was also admired by the Greeks.

of air, and at last it went out. Then the dawn light came quietly in, and lit the calm face, smiling wanly, a little tired, but deeply satisfied, under the white, drooping moustache.

That was the last evening of Charisis, the last tanner. When it was daylight, four men from the council, together with his friends, and the old women who had sat with him before, took him away.

The other things the papers said — such as calling him by the wrong name, and having him buried in the First Cemetery in Athens — are all lies. They were written by journalists who don't know any better.

That piper

For N. D. Triandaphyllopoulos

Apart from Zakynthos and Skiathos,[1] I don't know any other part of Greece that inspires one to read the poetry about its landscape. And as for Zakynthos, even after the earthquakes that destroyed the old town, the Hill of Strani and the Akrotiri remain, where, in spring, if you listen carefully and you have the gift, you will hear the "swooning airs and sounds not heard before".[2] But what is left in Skiathos of grandmother Skevo Yalinitsa, Phrangoyannou, and Moschoula?[3] This frail world, that every so often would say "Thanks be to God, we're saved again this time" — how can it withstand the disaster of development, that thinks nothing of dressing up the little port of Skiathos like a Tourkolimano,[4] with

---

[1] Skiathos was the birthplace of Alexandros Papadiamandis (1851–1911), Greece's much-loved and most eminent prose writer. There are many references in "That piper" to characters in his stories and Milionis has also quoted from them. The piper of the title is the shepherd in Papadiamandis' "The lament of the seal". The title also refers of course to Papadiamandis himself.

[2] "Swooning airs" echoes a line from "The free besieged", a long poem by Dionysios Solomos (1798–1857) who was born in Zakynthos, but moved to Corfu. He is generally regarded as the National Poet of Greece and the Greek national anthem consists of the first two stanzas of his "Hymn to Liberty".

[3] Characters from Papadiamandis stories: Skevo Yalinitsa appears in "Vardianos in quarantine"; Moschoula in "A dream among the waters" (in *Tales from a Greek island*, tr. Elizabeth Constantinides, Baltimore and London 1987); and Phrangouyannou in *The murderess* (tr. Peter Levi, London 1983, 1995; or tr. Liadain Sherrard, Limni, Evvia, 2011).

[4] Tourkolimano ("Turkish harbour') otherwise known as Mikrolimano ("small harbour") is a port near Piraeus largely devoted to tourism.

discos and coloured lights? The little port where Manos Koronios,[5] the skipper-fisherman, would moor his boat, where he slept a fitful sleep, tracing the Pleiades and all the mysteries of the heavens . . . Places for sin, those parts all around the port, where Polymnia's[6] wild violets grew, and on the charming hillocks with the umbrella pines and the olive trees, with the little churches and *koumbaros* Statharos' flock,[7] there are now cement bungalows — God Above! — and other tourist monstrosities. How can the delicate island withstand this invasion of contemporary barbarism? The Hill of Strani and the Akrotiri, that we mentioned before, are being guarded, for the moment, by the nobility of Zakynthos who occupy them; but the poor of Skiathos cannot be saved.

One understands now those people who have decided never to go to Skiathos, and who prefer to read about it in the pages of Papadiamandis. Their case reminds me of the story about Captain Nikolas, that an old Skiathian, uncle Odysseas, once told me.

"In my eighteenth year," he said, "I travelled to America. There, I joined a crew on a fishing boat. We fished for tuna. The captain came from our island, but hadn't set foot on it for about forty years. One time, he drew me aside and said, 'Heh, I wanted to ask you . . . That girl on the hill, near the Panayitsa Church, how's she getting on?'

"'What girl, Captain Nikola?'

---

[5] Koronios appears in Papadiamandis' story "The flower of the shore".
[6] Polymnia appears in Papadiamandis' story "All round the lake".
[7] *Koumbaros* can mean a godfather, a best man at a wedding, someone who helped a family in some way, or simply an esteemed friend. It can also be a general term of address for a friend or neighbour, as in the case of Statharos, in Papadiamandis' story "The Maidservant" (the name of a boat owned by a poor fisherman).

"'Ach, don't you know? ... The one who has the mulberry tree in the yard ...'

"After thinking a long while, I knew the woman he meant. 'But what *girl*, Captain?' I said to him. 'That one got married, and has children and grandchildren. She's an old woman now ...'

"'Ach!' he said, 'You're hopeless. You don't understand ...'

"And he went off. We didn't exchange another word the whole year I worked on the boat."

I'm telling this story again, not only because it was told me by a man who was old enough to have seen Papadiamandis with his own eyes — otherwise a reclusive figure for us today — but also because I believe that Papadiamandis would have told the story in his own particular way. As for uncle Odysseas, I had met him a few years ago, on a remote beach at Maliakos, near Achladi. He had come out of the sea, was drying himself in the sun, huddled in a corner, his whitish body a bag of bones like those bundles of roots that the sea has thrown up, and that have whitened on the summer sand — "abandoned driftwood, plunder, bleached relics of old, forgotten shipwrecks, telling mute tales of misfortune, and calamitous drownings" — as Papadiamandis would say. I sat beside him, and had a chat with him. He was a cheerful soul. An old seaman from Skiathos, he had ended up, through marriage, guarding Father Vasilis' orchards, opposite Lichada Lighthouse. A real Odysseus.

I was amazed that he could still swim, and asked him what age he was.

"I'm eighty-two," he replied proudly.

"Then you'll remember Papadiamandis," I remarked, without thinking.

"I remember him," he said, "with his beard. He was like a priest. He used to sing at the Church of the Three Bishops. And I remember them saying, 'That's Papadiamandis!'"

I calculated the years, and "expressed great surprise" when I confirmed that I really could have, before me, a person who had seen Papadiamandis with his own eyes. Until that moment, he was a very distant figure for me; of course I don't mean "with the angels above", but certainly within the boundaries of a fairy tale, a fairy tale that came, as they all do, from my childhood.

I remember when I heard my first story: it was "Children's Easter". My father read it to me, when he was coaching me in the top room of our house, before the Germans burned it — in the room where the window facing north was sealed up by the foliage of a large mulberry tree.

"My candle's better."

"No, mine is."

"*My* father chose it for me, and it is better."

"*My* mother decorated mine herself."

"And does your mother know how to *make* candles?"

I can still hear this children's dialogue, and I'm writing it now from memory. Was it *the magic of Papadiamandis?* But if poetry, like seed, is to take root, it is not enough for it to fall on the ground; the time has to be right as well. I was then in my second year at school. It was during the Occupation. The Secondary School was five hours away from our village. How it functioned in the midst of that calamity, I can't even remember. I only recall that I studied out of the sun, in shady places, and would go and sit examinations as "a pupil self-taught at home"; five hours on foot, from footpath to footpath, and forest to forest, so as not to come across German roadblocks. I can't say that we were hungry during the Occupation, but in the last months, before the harvest began, we were in serious difficulties. And the seasons, during those years, were contrary. It didn't rain. We had only frosts. Not even vegetables would grow. Nor did the birds lay eggs. At Easter, in '43, my mother went round the whole village, house by house, to find an egg — to dye it for me in the coffeepot, so that I could take it to the Resurrection ceremony. It was spring. The Resurrection ceremony was taking place at dawn, in a Byzantine monastery outside the village. The star shone high in the sky — the morning star, the planet Zeus[8] — the nightingales in the plane trees at the riverbeds enraptured us. A child's soul was open to every inspiring influence. With my Easter candle made from tallow, and my red egg, I said again, before the flickering flame, the words of Papadiamandis:

"My candle's better."

"No, mine is."

And then: "On Saturday evening, the crow will come, bringing cheese and meat. Then you'll see Evangelinos, full of joy, when he hears the crow going 'kra kra', and knocking on the window..." Of course, he didn't come. That summer, the Germans came and destroyed everything. Later, I read the other school stories: "The Lady's House", "The maidservant", "The gleaner" — "Neighbour Zerbinio expressed great surprise..." Thus began the bittersweet magic.

However, I didn't go to Skiathos until just last year, at Easter, even though my mind often wandered around her rose-coloured shores and terraces.

The sun was setting behind me, and, leaning on the gunwale, I had before me the prospect of the charming island of

---

[8] The Greek name for the planet Jupiter.

Tsoungria, and facing it, the island on which Papadiamandis portrayed the world.[9] And I confess that I felt an inexplicable delight, when, in a little while, the rock of Mavromandilou, the lady with the black kerchief, appeared, stooping into the sea. In the morning twilight, I saw her moving from afar, and beckoning to the presumptuous voyagers.

I had in my hand "Vardianos in quarantine", and I had only just read the first pages again. So, when the boat turned the headland to go into the port, I easily recognized Plakes, that stretched eight hundred feet into the water. It jutted out from the shore, a long neck in the sea, ending in three rocks: Megalos Kapparis, then Mytikas, and finally the lonely sea-girt Katergaki — tall rocks and sea-lashed marble. Between Plakes and Spilia, towards the east, was the Mathineï boatyard, and close to the rock, grandmother Skevo Yalinitsa's little house. I certainly couldn't see either the boatyard or the little house. But I happened to arrive at Skiathos at dusk, when imagination fills in what the eye cannot see.

Yet every day I was on the island, I leapt like Statharos' goats when I saw Papadiamandis in everything around me. Of course, it was necessary to leave behind me the Alkyon Hotel, the shop windows on the quay with their folksy souvenirs, and the tourists — even to leave behind his house, since one cannot be alone there, to ward off a deluge of discordant sounds, and to listen carefully in order to hear his voice — an effort like the one I had to make with Bephanis Lazos.

I was going down the road, one midday, from the church of Saint Charalambos, and I sat at the foot of an olive tree to have a rest. I saw a little old man walking towards me, with a light, almost skipping tread. He came over to me,

---

[9] The little island of Tsoungria was often used as a quarantine station.

asked me for a cigarette, squatted down beside me, and we began to chat. He had been gathering chicory, so as not to be a burden on his daughters-in-law, to whom he had left all his property, two hundred olive trees. He had no complaints, except that they didn't look after the trees. The world had changed. It had got used to the readymade. He also said he couldn't stop in one place. He liked to go around the countryside. If he stopped in one place, Charon would find him. That's why he made off, here and there, just like he escaped from the kitchens at Afyon Karahisar, when the Turks came in one door, and he slipped out the other, with the dishmop in his hand. Twelve years' military service at Sarandaporo, Kilkis, in Bessarabia — in the name of the law and Kondylis,[10] who gave as good as he got — in the Almyra Desert. Names that glittered in his rambling narration, and marked the erratic course of his life.

He smelt of ouzo. He took a small carafe out of the bag with the chicory in it, drank a mouthful, and, offered it to me. I asked him about Papadiamandis. "He was fond of a drink," he told me. He would drink with his father-in-law, Bephanis, and Lymberis, Chadzis, and Ikonomou — they drank at Lymberis' tavern. Ikonomou was a prosperous man, but he'd never put his hand in his pocket. They went one time to Xanemos to buy cucumber. Chiotis, the market-gardener, came out to them. "It's my own property now," he says to them. "*I* have it now." "Do you know," they said to him, "who this is? This is Papadiamandis."

With his finger, uncle Bephanis extinguished his cigarette in its woodbine holder. He blew the cigarette away, and went

---

[10] Colonel George Kondylis (1878–1936) took part in the struggle for Macedonia in 1916 and fought in the disastrous Asia Minor Campaign (1919–1922). Later he was a parliamentarian and twice prime minister for brief periods.

tripping off down to the olive-grove — a man of limited understanding — just like the rest of us. I walked behind him, putting together his phrases, taking words from here and there, from the remarks that came higgledy-piggledy, almost incomprehensibly, out of his toothless mouth, breathing ouzo fumes, remarks tangled up with names of places in the Balkans and Asia Minor. But in the end, look, "Parisis' fig orchard"[11] and Xanemos "where the north wind holds sway".

This is more or less the way I read Papadiamandis — in forgotten corners of the upper quarter of the town, in shady olive-groves, in bright meadows, on the sea-worn rocks. And in the end, the same things spoke to me in his language. And don't tell me that it was fantasy, an obsession, and that in Skiathos, there's nothing left but Lalaria for the tourists; we would have to go back again to the pedantic problem of whether the truth is found within us or outside us. And I didn't go to Skiathos to solve problems, rather to let my own eyes see what my heart desired.

Reason said within me, give to the heart what it desires.[12]

I certainly didn't find, anywhere around the port, Polymnia's wild violets, perfuming the air with their fragrance.[13]

The truth is that I didn't look very hard. Instead, I visited Mnimouria many times. On the crosses, I read the names, Mathinos, Yalis, Lymberis, Phragoulas. I had a chat with an old woman, a gossip, who was washing the railings and

---

[11] Parisis appears in Papadiamandis' story "All round the lake".
[12] From the poem "Apokopos" by Bergadis (16th century).
[13] In "All around the lake" the young men gather wild violets for the lovely Polymnia.

weeding the grave of Adamandios,[14] priest and *ikonomos*,[15] and his wife. "Those who behold this tomb, pray for them." I looked over the top of the hill, "down whose slopes have rolled ceaselessly towards the sea that receives all" — and were still rolling down — "bits of rotten wood, and bones of the disinterred, fragments of gold shoes, or the gold embroidered petticoats of young women."[16] I went down the slope to the boatyard. And I tried to get to Kochyli, by the other side of the hill, but the path that Akrivoula[17] would have taken was being guarded by a black dog.

Finally, one evening, when I was coming from the west, on the road that goes to Koukounaries, there suddenly rose up in front of me the hill with the cypress trees, bathed in the dazzling sun as it was setting, "its rays caressing the little orchard, and the spotless, whitewashed tombs that glowed in those last rays".[18]

It was just after rain. A special moment. In the calm of the evening, I clearly heard the flute of that rare, matchless piper, playing the lament of the seal.[19]

It was my last day on Skiathos.

---

[14] The father of Alexandros Papadiamandis.
[15] An honorary title bestowed on married priests, who are not permitted to become bishops.
[16] These lines are taken from Papadiamandis' description of the graveyard (*Mnimouria*) on Skiathos in the story "The lament of the seal".
[17] A little girl who drowns in "The lament of the seal".
[18] A quotation from "The lament of the seal".
[19] In the story an old fisherman, who knows the silent language of seals, interprets the lament of the seal as a lament for the death of Akrivoula.

From generation to generation

When I happen sometimes to be in the company of "scholars" — to use a term that, for most people, is rather outdated — who are older than I am, and I hear them saying "our generation", I immediately go into my shell, hunching my shoulders and shrinking further into my chair. This phrase must surely be a chronological classification, and nothing more, since the people who say this are older than me by about ten years. Yet the phrase is rarely spoken in a neutral tone. Most times, it is uttered with emphasis, which, according to the occasion, takes on a nuance of dramatization, or even arrogance, especially when one of these people addresses me personally, and says "my generation". In the second instance, I imagine, it is to be understood that he is the defending champion of ideological and philological contests[2] — often the two become entangled, and one cannot distinguish between them — while in the first instance, are clearly implied the sufferings that uphold a

TITLE. The Greek title, *En yenea ke yenea* (three syllables with the stress on the last: *ye-ne-á*), is from Psalm 90, verse 1, in the Septuagint, a Greek translation of the Jewish Bible (the Christian Old Testament) made in Alexandria, Egypt, in the last three centuries BC and used by the Greek Orthodox Church (Psalm 89.1 in Western Bibles). The whole verse translates as "Lord, you have been our refuge *in generation and generation*". More frequent in the Psalms is the related expression *eis yenean ke yenean* ("unto generation and generation"); and a number of other variants occur, including *apo yeneas eis yenean* at Psalm 9.27 (10.6) which provides the English title, "From generation to generation".

[2] The purist language or *katharevousa* (making Greek more like Ancient Greek) tended to be imposed on educational institutions by right-wing governments while *dimotiki* (the language of the people) was favoured by the left wing. *Katharevousa* was the official language of the Greek State until it was replaced by *dimotiki* in 1976.

"maimed", "belied", "dispersed" — in a word, "lost" generation.

I don't mean — in other words I mustn't generalise — that circumstances have not also arisen when my contemporaries played a leading role in our struggles, and were brutally tortured, especially during the period of the dictatorship,[3] and that they can't speak as equals to the first group we were referring to, and become "at one" with them in the end. But I fear that these are precisely the exceptions that prove the rule, as we say. We, the others, most of us, will have to make up our minds that we have proved ourselves unworthy to be registered in this contemporary *Libro d'Oro*,[4] which, if it doesn't ensure privilege — you don't worry about what privilege — nevertheless relieves you, at least, of that burden that weighs on you like guilt — a somewhat traumatic situation, that can warp your behaviour, making it unnatural.

I remember one evening, during the dictatorship, I was invited with my friends to S's house, a mutual friend of ours who worked on the ships, so that we could talk "among ourselves", and sing a song or two, and relax. An indispensable member of our company is K, of another age group, another "category", as they used to say at the time when people were classified during mobilisation. He once had a teaching post, and now, as an almost free-lance teacher, he has scarcely time to rush by taxi from Chalandri to Kypseli to give lessons. To us, K is a treasure, because,

---

[3] This refers to the period of military rule (the Junta) 1967–1974, though there were earlier periods of dictatorship during the 20th century.
[4] "The Book of Gold": a register which existed in several Italian cities, as well as in Venetian Corfu and Crete, in which the names of noble families were inscribed in letters of gold.

apart from knowing all the tavernas, from high-class ones, and "stamping-grounds", to various "dives", he is a real living history book. He lived through all the post-war events, and, unlike us, he lived them actively — in ELAS as a partisan, in the Civil War, in prisons, and on Makronisos.[5] As he is also, indeed, an excellent narrator, we hang on his every word, especially at those times when wine clouds the brain and carries you away. Then our eyes glaze over, and our faces become flushed. "You should write that down, K," we tell him, when — in a bitter mood — he finishes the story, and bangs his glass down on the table. "Nobody could have told it like that." Then he draws circles in the air with his hand, and purses his lips. "What do you want to remind me of that for? You've upset me again." For us, indeed, K is a man "of myth", and at those times, he assumes his true dimensions. At other times, he is not only ordinary, but less than ordinary.

Anyway, on the evening at S's house, we had a surprise: S had brought along a Yugoslav seaman, called Vlado, a very tall man, about six and a half feet. Naturally, S gave him the seat of honour, one of the two armchairs, beside the small table with the drinks. The rest of us made ourselves comfortable any way we could on the chairs and the stool. We discussed the situation, giving the Junta various time limits, and then we started singing — S plays the guitar well — Theodorakis[6] to begin with, and then, at last, an old

---

[5] The island of Makronisos, lying off the east coast of Attica, was a notoriously brutal prison camp, used by the Junta (and at other times) to intern political opponents.

[6] Mikis Theodorakis (born 1925) is a composer who has set to music works of the major poets of Greece, notably Seferis, Elytis and Ritsos. He has always been associated with the Left (though in recent years he has been more concerned with reconciliation between political groups). His music was banned during the Junta period.

ELAS partisan song that we all, of course, remember from childhood. During an interval, S made Vlado tell us, in his broken Greek, about the People's Republic of Yugoslavia, and about the Serbian civil war. He had been a partisan with Tito. "Did you know, Vlado," S said to him at one moment, "that K was a partisan too." "Yes, indeed," said K, and he quietly slid off the stool where he was sitting, until that moment, and scrambled into the second armchair that had remained vacant beside the Yugoslav, and that none of us, as was taken for granted at the time, had dared to touch. We were at a loss. We stopped singing, and looked at them talking quietly to each other about "their experiences". You could have said that our evening was almost spoiled. In vain, S kept strumming his introductory notes on the guitar, and beginning the first words of the song himself. At last, he got fed up, and abandoned the attempt. The discussion degenerated into chat, and this too was carried on among small groups of us, until we finally looked at our watches, and remembered that "we must go" and that "we have to get up early for work".

A more extreme case — and for this reason perhaps, more characteristic — is F, also a contemporary. When the rebels were active,[7] he was always to be found at the front of demonstrations, running, dishevelled, his eyes red with tear gas. We were always saying that at any minute, they would beat him up, and he would lose his job. The man is a clerk. And he would escape from them every time. There he would

---

[7] This refers to the demonstrations of 1965 and 1966 in support of George Papandreou and against King Constantine. The largest demonstration took place in July 1965 when the King forced Papandreou to resign as prime minister. These events were a prelude to the military takeover of 1967.

be, coming to our rendezvous at midnight to bring us the news. It was in the period of the dictatorship that he took the bit between his teeth. During the Polytechnic revolt[8] we lost sight of him for three days and nights. Somebody said they might have seen him on Friday evening, making a speech at a corner, somewhere around Alexandras Avenue and Mavromateon Street, but they couldn't be sure. The fact is that he came back to us on Sunday, pale and distressed, and told us excitedly about "the young people". Again, K made that characteristic gesture, drawing circles in the air with his hand, his lips pursed. "Here's to us," he said with a fatalistic sigh, and banged his glass down on the table, which incensed F, who turned on him: "You lot never will acknowledge anything, except what you've done yourselves." Worst of all, he added: "And come to think of it, what did you do actually? What was the result? Like a cow that fills the churn with milk, and then gives it a kick, and overturns it." It was another evening spoiled with "you lot".

Finally, since we've started, it would perhaps be worth mentioning the case of A, who is the most restrained among our company, the calmest of us, and, I would say, the one who is most sure of his position. I certainly don't mean his government post — he's a teacher — but his other position. He came from a family that gave a lot, and suffered a lot. He himself escaped, but not without hardship, most of which was bureaucratically inflicted. He passed right under their noses, came out on top, and achieved material stability at

---

[8] On the 14th of November 1973 students marched on and occupied the Athens Polytechnic to demonstrate against the Junta. Three days later the revolt was put down with great brutality. There were several deaths and large numbers of injured (the figures remain a matter of dispute), and this event turned the tide of opinion decisively against the Junta.

last, but more importantly, an inner stability. Without ceasing to "live" events, he raises them to an intellectual level, avoiding "fruitless gestures". The two of us often get together, and try to find "a way out" among theoretical meanderings and other concepts. So, one evening, during the dictatorship, we took refuge in a joint in Kato Patisia, in Patmou Street, if I remember correctly. It was a basement place, run by a man who was blind in one eye. He and his elderly wife came from Epirus. We were from the same province. He served only salted codfish and black haricot beans with vinegar. At first, there were just the two of us. Then some young people came in, with long hair, beards, and frayed jeans. They were noisy. In a while, however, they all sang a quiet song together with a guitar: "On the secret shore" and "Intelligible sun of Justice".[9] They must have been students. We stopped our discussion, and listened with delight. I took a paper napkin, and wrote on it:

> *Well do we eat and drink and sing our people's songs.*
> *Are we not doing something good, good for our own souls?*
> *We'll go and take the bridge, the bridge that stands at Tricha,*
> *where Voïvondas passes with the men in chains.*[10]

I passed it discreetly over to their table. It took a bit of imagination to understand what I meant by these lines, which are from another age, but it seems that during difficult times, people's sensitivity to messages is more acute. The young people understood it. They all raised their glasses to us. They sent us a half litre of wine, and then began to sing more daring songs. We got excited too, and, forgetting what

---

[9] Theodorakis' settings of the poem "Denial" by George Seferis and lines from the *Axion Esti* of Odysseas Elytis.
[10] From an old klephtic ballad, dating from the Ottoman period. Voïvondas was a Turkish general. By implication the lines here refer to those imprisoned by the Junta.

times we were living in, joined in the singing. At one moment, one of the young people, with long hair and a beard, got up from his seat, came over to us, and said in a severe tone: *If I'm not mistaken, you're a teacher.* A turned pale, and stammered something between yes and no. *And if I'm not mistaken,* he continued, *you are A.* This time, A did not reply. He just looked at him with glazed eyes, full of pleading and fear. Fortunately, the young man abandoned the game, and introduced himself. They were all old pupils of his, unrecognizable now. Of course, cordialities and the rest followed, but it was as if a glass had broken. Because it's no small thing to be brought down to size by one of your pupils.

The examples I have mentioned are clear-cut, and belong in the area of the conscious. Searching, with a little care, you can find a mass of instances where the subconscious shows its ugly face. And not only in our everyday behaviour, but also in our literary works, at least those that were written or will be written, with sincerity, at moments, that is, when the writer comes face to face with events, and has not permitted himself to benefit from the blood of others, with guile and deceit. Besides, only in this way are genuine works written. I mention, only as an example, the verses of a contemporary poet, who, speaking about homosexuals, says:

as they hunt the leftists, so they hunt us, my brothers[11]

a simile which, if my psychological capabilities don't deceive me, reveals what the poet would prefer to be.

In the end, I don't know if we are really guilty or not, since nobody chooses the hour when they were born. Because I imagine — or I hope — that what defined our

---

[11] From a poem by Dinos Christianopoulos (1931–2020).

characters was the era in which we were born. When things happened around us that "the others", those older than us, call "cosmogony", we weren't old enough to see their deeper, their real dimensions. Then came the years when not only did they not offer themselves for heroic deeds, but they did not even offer reflections, which could have been marked by those burning prefixes — the "crypto-", and "philo-", or even the so-called, naïve "supporters of".[12] These were indelibly stamped on you, like the number on the arm of a Jew — and then, suppose you have the face to go afterwards and "put your cards on the table". The only certainty would be inglorious humiliation.

That's how things were, until the same things happened to us the second time. Almost "imperceptibly",[13] as the poet would say, the young ones were suddenly among us. Timorously at first, then more boldly, they too began to talk about "our generation" — the generation of the Polytechnic. It's true that these, although they haven't the self-complacency, or the dramatic tone of the first post-war generation, have a certainty — the innocents — a quiet certainty that hits the ear-drum more painfully. Because these were almost children, and you, the mature person, who should have been "ready and willing" . . . and so on. And when you can't find justice, why should others do it for you?

The only thing that remains now, beyond the *mea culpa*, is for us to say "our generation", and for no other reason than not to be without a name and altogether annihilated, invisible, unheard of — a generation lost, in the literal sense of the word.

---

[12] The Security Police referred to leftists who were not members of the Communist Party as "crypto-communists" or "philo-communists".
[13] An allusion to the poem "Walls" by C. P. Cavafy: "imperceptibly they have shut me off from the world outside".

AN ALPHABETICAL LIST OF GREEK PERSONAL AND PLACE NAMES AND OTHER GREEK WORDS, WITH THE STRESSED SYLLABLES MARKED

The following alphabetical list includes all the Greek personal and place names that occur in this book (in the main text and in some footnotes), and a few other Greek words (with no initial capital). Each name or other word is divided into syllables and the stressed syllable is printed in bold type.

Where names are followed by (AG) = Ancient Greek, (L) = Latin, or (E) = English, the stress is placed where it usually falls when the words are pronounced by English speakers. In these names the sound values outlined for Modern Greek on pages x–xii do not necessarily apply. In some cases the translator has preferred the Ancient Greek forms to the modern, most significantly in the case of Acheron (stress on the first syllable) where the modern demotic Greek name is Acherondas (stress on the second syllable). Names belonging to other languages and countries (Albania and Hungary for example) are not included in this list unless they appear in distinctively Greek forms. Some of the best known place names in Greece are not listed here either and appear in the text in their usual English forms (Athens, Corfu, Corinth, Epirus, Rhodes, etc.), as do a few personal names (e.g. Rebecca, George, Constantine).

Syllable division follows English rather than Greek practice. Where double consonants occur they are split between two syllables (e.g. **Yan**-nis) but this does not imply that the repeated letter is pronounced twice. It is just that the alternatives look too odd to use (e.g. **Ya**-nnis or **Yann**-is).

It should be noted that when an unstressed I comes between a consonant and another vowel it often does not have full syllabic value, but constitutes a brief transition from consonant to vowel similar to the insertion of a non-vocalic Y. The English word *colonial*, for example is not usually pronounced as four full syllables, co-**lo**-ni-al, but more often as co-**lo**-nyal).

ALPHABETICAL LIST OF GREEK PERSONAL AND PLACE NAMES

A-che-ron (AG)
A-che-rou-**si**-a
Ach-**la**-di
A-da-**man**-di-os
Ak-ri-**vou**-la
Ak-ro-**ti**-ri
A-le-**xan**-dras (Avenue)
A-**le**-xan-dros
Al-e-**xo**-pou-los
A-li-**ou**-sis
A-**li**-pa-sas
Al-ky-**on**
Al-my-**ra**
A-na-dy-**o**-me-ne (AG)
An-**thou**-po-lis
A-**pel**-les (AG)
A-phro-**di**-te (AG)
A-**po**-ko-pos
A-**ra**-cho-va
Ar-**yi**-re-na
Ar-yi-**ro**-kas-tro
Ar-**yi**-ris
As-tros
A-**thi**-na
A-**ve**-roph
A-**yi**-a
A-yi-os
Be-lo-**yan**-nis
Be-**pha**-nis
Ber-**ga**-dis
Bin-dos
Boe-o-ti-a (L)
Bou-na
Ca-**va**-fy (E)
Chad-**zis**

Cha-**lan**-dri
Cha-**ra**-lam-bos
Cha-**rik**-lei-a
Cha-**ri**-sis
Cha-ron (AG)
Chi-**o**-tis
Chris-ti-a-**no**-pou-los
Chris-**to**-pho-ros
Cni-dus (L)
Cre-on (AG)
Dae-da-lus (L)
Del-**phi**
De-**ro**-po-lis
Di-**mit**-ri-os
Di-**mit**-ris
di-mo-ti-**ki**
Di-nos
Di-o-**ny**-si-os
Dou-li-as
Dri-nos
Dry-i-**nou**-po-li
Ec-**ba**-ta-na (E)
E-**ly**-tis
E-ri-mos
E-van-ge-li-**nos**
E-van-**thi**-a
flo-**ka**-ti (E)
Gad-zi-**o**-ris
Ga-ki-as
Ga-kis
Gon-dos
Gou-si-**a**-ro
Gou-**yan**-nos
Gram-mos
Gri-bo-**yan**-nis

107

He-ra (AG)
Her-cu-les (L)
Hyd-ra (AG)
i-ko-**no**-mos
I-ko-**no**-mou
I-**lei**-a
Ip-po-**kra**-tous (Street)
Ka-ka-vi-**a**
Ka-la-**mas**
Kam-**bi**-lis
Kap-pa-ris
Ka-**phi**-ris
Ka-ra-**bi**-nas
Ka-ra-tha-**na**-sis
Ka-si-di-**a**-ris
Kas-**ta**-ni-a-ni
Kas-tri-**o**-tis
Kas-tro
Ka-ter-**ga**-ki
ka-tha-**re**-vou-sa
Ka-to
Kat-**sou**-lis
Kil-**kis**
Kit-sos
Kla-**da**-ki
Klei-**sou**-ra
Ko-**chy**-li
Ko-las
Kol-li-as
kol-ly-va
Kon-da-**xis**
Kon-**dy**-lis
Ko-ri-an-do-**li**-no
Ko-**ro**-ni-os
Kos-tas
Kou-kou-na-ri-**es**

koum-**ba**-ros
Kou-ram-**bas**
Kour-man-i-**o**
Kri-tha-ro-**pa**-za-ro
Ky-nou-**ri**-a
Kyp-**se**-li
La-ka
La-**la**-ri-a
Lav-da-ni
La-zos
Le-che-**na**
Le-na
Ler-na (AG)
Le-o-ni-das (AG)
Li-**a**-bi
Li-**bo**-cho-vo
Li-**cha**-da
Lim-nos
Lon-dos
Lym-**be**-ris
Ma-chos
Mak-**ro**-ni-sos
Mak-ry-**no**-ros
Ma-li-a-**kos**
Ma-nos
Man-thos
Ma-ri-**an**-thi
Mar-ga-**ri**-ta
Ma-**ri**-na
Ma-thi-**ne**-ï
Ma-thi-**nos**
Mav-ro-man-di-**lou**
Mav-ro-ma-**te**-on (Street)
Me-**ga**-lo / Me-**ga**-los
mel-**te**-mi
Mer-min-gas

ALPHABETICAL LIST OF GREEK PERSONAL AND PLACE NAMES

Me-ta-**xas**
Met-so-vo
Mi-**cha**-lis
Mi-kis
Mik-ro-**li**-ma-no
Mi-li-**o**-nis
Mi-**nas**
mi-ro-**lo**-yi
mi-ro-**lo**-yi-a
Mit-ros
Mit-sos
Mi-ya
Mni-**mou**-ri-a
Mo-ly-**va**-da
Mo-ly-**va**-des
Mo-**re**-a / Mo-**re**-an (E)
Mos-**chou**-la
Mour-**ga**-na
Mou-**zi**-na
My-ti-kas
Na-po-**le**-on
Ne-**mert**-si-ka
Ni-**ko**-las
Ni-kos
O-dys-**se**-as
O-**dys**-seus (AG)
o-**ka**(s)
O-**lyt**-si-ka
Pa-na-**yit**-sa
Pa-pa-di-a-**man**-dis
Pa-pa-di-mi-tra-**ko**-pou-los
Pa-pan-**dre**-ou
Pa-**ri**-sis
Par-nas-**sos**
Pa-**ti**-si-a
Pat-mou (Street)

Pav-**la**-kos
pei-na
Pe-le-pon-**nese** (E)
Per-di-**ka**-ri
Per-**se**-pho-ne (AG)
Pe-**trou**-po-lis
Pha-**na**-ri
Phe-zos
Phi-**los**-tra-tos (AG)
Phle-si-as
Phlo-ri-na
Phou-**se**-kis
Phra-**gou**-las
Phran-go-yan-**nou**
Phry-ni
Phry-ne (AG)
Pi-**rae**-us (L)
Pla-kes
Plei-a-des (AG)
Plu-to (L)
Po-**go**-ni-a
Po-**lym**-ni-a
Por-tar-i-**a**
Pra-**xi**-te-les (AG)
Rap-ti / **Rap**-tis
Re-ma
Rit-sos
Rou-ve-las
Sa-be-**tha**-ï
Sa-ran-**da**-po-ro
Sar-**ris**
Sen-**gou**-nas
Se-**fe**-ris (E)
Si-a-man-**da**-kas
Si-**ë**-mos
Si-**ou**-las

ALPHABETICAL LIST OF GREEK PERSONAL AND PLACE NAMES

Sken-**de**-ris
Ske-vo
Ski-**a**-thi-an (E)
Ski-**a**-thos
So-lo-**mos**
Sou-li
Spar-ta (L)
Spi-li-**a**
Spy-ri-don
Spy-ros
Sta-tha-**ros**
Sta-**mou**-lis
Stra-ni
Stra-tis
sym-**pho**-ni-se
Ta-chi-dro-**mei**-a
Te-pe-**le**-ni
Te-ta
The-o-do-**ra**-kis
Ther-**mo**-py-lae (L)
Thes-sa-lo-**ni**-ki
Thes-pi-ae (L)
Tho-**do**-ra
Tho-do-**re**-los
Tho'-**re**-los
Ti-le-gra-**phi**-a
Ti-**le**-pho-na
Ti-**ta**-ni-a
To-lis
Tour-ko-**li**-ma-no
Tri-an-da-phyl-**lo**-pou-los
Tri-an-**da**-phyl-los
Tri-cha
Try-**go**-na
tsa-mi-ko

Tsoun-gri-**a**
Val-tis-ta
Van-**ge**-lis
Var-di-**a**-nos
Va-ri-**a**-des
Va-si-li-**ki**
Va-**si**-lis
Va-**si**-lo
Va-si-o
Vi-to
Vla-**chei**-dis
Vla-chos
Vla-do
Vo-ï-von-das
Ya-li-**nit**-sa
Ya-lis
Yan-nis
Yan-nos
Yan-ne-na
Ya-ros
Ye-**ro**-the-os
Yo-**an**-nis
Yo-te-na
Xa-ne-mos
Xer-xes (E)
Za-**go**-ri-a
Za-kyn-thos
Zer-bi-ni-**o**
Zer-vas
Zeus (AG)
zi-**am**-ba
Zi-kos
Zo-ïs
Zo-si-**me**-a

Lightning Source UK Ltd.
Milton Keynes UK
UKHW041617200521
384059UK00002B/40